The Known &
Unknown
Sea

Alan Bilton

Cillian Press |

First published in Great Britain in 2014
by Cillian Press Limited. 83 Ducie Street, Manchester M1 2JQ
www.cillianpress.co.uk

British Library Cataloguing in Publication Data.
A catalogue record for this book is available from the British Library.

Paperback ISBN: 978-1-909776-02-9
eBook ISBN: 978-1-909776-03-6

Published by
Cillian Press – Manchester - 2014
www.cillianpress.co.uk

For Pamela and Laurie

Contents

The Bay of Seething

1

The day the tickets arrived, our whole family gathered around my grandfather's table to decide *what should be done*. The mood was tense. Mum had already got to work packing, but my three grannies "clucked like chickens near the pot" (Dad). "Why go, why set sail?" asked Granny Mair. "Get on a strange boat, go across the water – but for what?" Granny Dwyn agreed. "The sea is no feather bed!" "And Alex is such a delicate child," said Auntie Glad, shaking her spoon at me. "Just at look at that pup – trust me, that is not a boy who'll float." I had eaten huge amounts of jelly and was bouncing up and down on Uncle Glyn's lap. "Will it be a very big boat?" I asked, flapping my arms like a bird. "Oh very, very big," said Uncle Glyn. "Why if everyone in the town were to go on deck, there would still be room for a friend." "And is it a long way from one end to the other?" I asked. "A long way?" Uncle Glyn poked me in the belly. "Why, if you set off in the morning, you'd have grown a beard before you got half way." Ah, how big and strange the world was – and how awfully close to boot. "And is it also very high?" I asked. "My child," said Uncle Glyn, patting me on my puffy cheeks, "if you put a ladder on the top you'd scrape the sky with your hat." "Glyn, don't fill his head with nonsense," said my dad. "The lad's as stupid as a goose as it is." Dad stared at the tabletop like it was a trapdoor about to open. He agreed with Granny Dwyn and Auntie Glad: no good could come of this! I closed my eyes and counted to ten but when I opened them again the tickets were still there. They were a lovely sky-blue colour, the same as my bedroom. "You think all that water will keep you up?" said Granny Dwyn. "A fish can't swim in soup..."

The tickets had arrived the day before, delivered by some little fella in a "suspicious looking" van. The envelope had no stamp and the guy who came to the door "wasn't even a real postman" (my brother) – he was dressed all in white and came to the door with an enormous moustache. When he rang the doorbell, Mum was listening to sad music and sighing, but as soon as she tore open the envelope, the colour raced back to her cheeks. "Go and find your water-wings," she said. "And maybe your sun-hat too." My brother, the legalist, picked up the letter and started to go through the small print, but Mum was already on the phone to Aunt Bea, her "mercury steadily rising" (Dad). Amazingly Aunt Bea had won tickets too – mother's cheeks were hot and wet. "Alex, change the record will you?" Mum cried. "This is no time for tears!" I could hear Aunt Bea bawling and my mother laughing and I joined in by beating the table with a stick. "But we didn't even enter a competition," complained my brother, who, despite the excitement still wanted "proof" and "facts"; he had an awfully angry look on his face and waved the envelope under our noses accusingly. Mum wasn't listening though; instead she gathered clothes from all round the house, piling them up in one enormous heap. "Have we been burgled or is your mother cleaning?" (Dad). When he came home, my father picked up the tickets, scrunched up his eyes, and carefully inspected the paperwork through his "skepticals". "We've been to no travel agent, filled in no form, entered no raffle…" he said. Mum didn't care. "If someone bakes you a cake, do you ask to check the recipe?" My father and brother looked at each other with the same melancholy expression while I kept hitting the table with a stick.

Meanwhile news of the tickets was spreading fast. Envelopes had been distributed from Windy Harbour Road to Nant Celyn, but not everyone had been so lucky it seemed. Some people had won tickets but others had not, just like the sheep and the goats, or some such thing. To the untrained eye there seemed neither rhyme nor reason. Publicans, council-workers, butchers, estate agents – some had received sky-blue envelopes, others *zip*. "But why haven't I been chosen?" cried Mrs Griffith in the Post Office, tears rolling down her cheeks. "Who gets to decide?" No one had an answer. "This will come to a bad end," said Mr McAuley, who ran the newsagent. "You don't measure your collar size by putting your neck in a noose." Mr and Mrs McAuley hadn't received any tickets and eyed up their customers suspiciously. "There now," said Mrs Crowther, in a vain attempt to cheer Mrs Griffith up. "See! The newsagent will still be open, and the fish shop too." But Mrs Griffith kept on crying. "It hurts here," she said, pointing either to her heart or to her shoulder, it wasn't very clear. Oh, for pity! Oh, for shame! Looking at her made you want to cry too, especially if you didn't have a ticket either.

Of course many considered the tickets to be a hoax; "Nobody gets something for nothing this side of the grave," hissed Mrs Keenan, stroking her cat. And yet, everything *looked* official: accommodation, meals, paid excursions, passage to the other side. My brother and I asked Granny Dwyn about what lay on the other shore of the bay, but she just slapped our arms and snapped, "There is no other side!" and that was that.

Even so, dozens of people (my brother and I amongst them) rushed down to the seafront to see what could be seen. Unfortunately, it was pretty disappointing: drizzle, emptiness, the bay shrouded in mist, "from here to the front steps of eternity" (Uncle Tomos). No matter how hard you looked, you still couldn't see the other shore – only vague shapes and blobs, like the view through Granny Mair's glasses. A fair sized crowd gathered on the front but there wasn't much to get excited about. "Like staring into the inside of a hat!" (Cousin George). My brother and I went there on our bikes after seeing Granny Dwyn, but by the time we got there it was dark and there was even less to see than before. What was fog anyway? Fold after fold of nothingness. Yet somehow we were to go there…

In our house it was decided that we should all meet in Grandfather's front room, as he had the biggest table, albeit not necessarily the cleanest. "To what do I owe this honour?" grumbled Grandy, curved like a teacher's cane. ("Guests are like tacks," he muttered, "easy to get hammered, impossible to get out.") Grandy, Grandy, old and bent/counting the cost/of a life mis-spent! Strangely I had three grandmothers but only one grandfather, and I could never work out which one he belonged too. The three grannies all wore black and sat together like a tea-cosy with three spouts – Granny Dwyn, Granny Mair, and the other one. Grandpa sat on his own, "stewing in his juices" (my mother). He smoked his pipe and watched people traipsing in and out of his kitchen. "The fattest sow is first in line at the trough!" The house was full of cousins and half-cousins and cousins-by second marriage – "magpies in the family tree!" (Granny Dwyn). I had to call anyone higher than the sideboard 'Auntie' or 'Uncle', which was awfully confusing. It was also very busy. Chairs were squeezed into Grandy's front room, and when it was completely full, more chairs were squeezed on top. "Mind the paintwork!" Grandy bellowed but nobody was listening. Instead, everyone stared at the sky-blue tickets on the table. "Just like the colour of my bedroom," I whispered to my brother, but he just rolled his eyes and rested his saucer of biscuits on my head.

"The important thing," said my father, "is that we consider things sensibly, don't get carried away with a lot of wild talk…" But you know what they say – you might as well try shouting down the gas pipe; the men all wanted to talk about boats and the women all wanted to talk about packing. According to the letter, only two cases per person were permitted, and this was the cause of much consternation. What about hand luggage? Could children be assigned two cases too? And what should be packed: summer dresses, warm coats, a scarf and hat for the sea voyage? Aunt Bea would go nowhere without her navy ball gown. "It's my one chance to wear it out!" Others felt that waterproofs and a stout so-wester were a better bet. "Just look at all that fog," they argued. "You expect to get a tan from *mist*?" There were other things to be considered too: plants to be watered, lawns to be tended, pets to be looked after. "Bury me in my garden," said Granny Dwyn. "At least I'll be able to keep an eye on the beans." Grandpa's larder was pretty much empty by now. "Why not take the furniture and the light fittings too?" he bellyached, hiding his best biscuits. By this stage in proceedings the action had started to move away from Grandfather's enormous table and was beginning to spill out to the front room. Cousins I hardly recognised were chasing each other harum-scarum around the furniture, whilst others formed a line of stepping-stones from Grandpa's cushions. Grandpa's brows knitted together to form one thick continuous line. "Where did these pups grow up, a farm yard?" he yelled. I hid beneath the legs of Grandpa's famous table and emptied jelly out into a shoe.

"The letter doesn't even say how long the trip's for, or how long it will take to get there," said Dad. "How are we supposed to plan for anything?"

"That man!" hissed Mum. "He'd be miserable drowning in ice

cream." Recently my mother had taken to standing in doorways and sighing. My brother blamed this on the books she read, which were Russian and tragic.

Afterwards an argument broke out about visa regulations but then somebody put on some music and Aunt Bea and Mum started to dance.

"Do you think the fog will lift?" asked Uncle Huw, cleaning out his ear. "I don't see how the boat will be able to dock otherwise…"

"Fog," I sang. "Fog, fog, fog…"

"Ah, they know what they're doing," said Uncle Glyn, picking up the envelope. "Just look at that lettering!"

"And the paper – so thick!"

"Pff, boats, tickets, envelopes," said Granny Dwyn, peering through the curtains. "You might as well set sail for the moon…"

Away from Granddad's table the party was getting out of hand. There were cousins everywhere. Cake was trampled underfoot. "Like a herd of elephants!" thundered Grandy. Mum closed her eyes and started to sing along to the music – something about a stranger and love and the moon. My brother looked at me sternly. "It's those books!" he whispered. "That's why she breathes funny too."

Then it was time to go. Nothing had been decided. Nobody knew who was going and who was staying. Auntie Glad burst into tears on the doorstep and Grandy shouted "Women: the world's sorrow!" and went back in to check on his sherry. I was sitting on his famous table, drawing pictures of monsters on a napkin. "Little monkey!" Grandy growled. Father was deep in thought. "Or deep in something!" (Uncle Glyn). There was a brief moment of panic when we all thought that our tickets were missing, but after a short search they turned up safe and sound, under a scrunched-up napkin. "You'd do better to toss them out with the rest of the rubbish," said Granny Dwyn. Her round old face looked like an owl chewing a mouse. The three grannies all left together in a taxi so I still didn't know which one Grandpa belonged to. Outside it was gloomy and grey. Fog was massing in the west, like a heavy curtain spread across the street. The sky felt very close, like it was just above our heads. "Fog, fog, fog," I yelled. When we got back to our house night fell like an axe.

2

The day after the confab around Grandfather's famous table was a school day, so my brother and I put on our uniforms and cycled there as normal. It was a Tuesday: my brother had a maths exam and I had to paint a picture of fish. But half way through Craft, Miss Evans stood up at the front of the class and announced that any child who has received a ticket could leave straight away. "No reason to stay on now…"

The room went very quiet – "quiet as the Queen's farts" (Cousin Ieuan). Not a child moved whilst Miss Evans' eyes passed over the kids like a searchlight.

"Children?"

I did my best to sink down behind the desk but it was no use.

Alex, did *you* get a ticket?"

"Yes Miss…"

"Well, off you go then. And don't forget your coat…"

All the kids were staring at me, their little round faces as pale as mushrooms. No one said a word. Above me the strip light buzzed like a wasp.

"Alex? Come on Alex, let's go…"

As soon as I went out into the corridor I smelt a strong chemically-smell – maybe bleach, maybe something else. The corridor was silent. As I passed each classroom I could hear various lessons going on, but out in the hallway: nothing. How strange it all was – like I'd fallen through the cracks into someplace else entirely.

Luckily Michael was waiting for me over by the bike shed. Oh Mikey! We should have been really happy but we both looked kind of dazed. "I didn't even do my test," he sighed, throwing his school bag up on his back. As we pushed our bikes out, the school felt very small, like something you could pick up and carry home in your pocket. No bell tolled. There weren't any other kids around *anywhere*.

"Mikey?" I said. "How come nobody else has got a ticket?"

Mikey looked at me sadly and shook his head.

"Mikey?"

"Come on Alex," he said. "Let's get on our bikes and go…"

The road down from our school ran alongside the park and the play-area where I'd once got lost despite the fact that it was *mathematically impossible* (Mikey), then down the steep hill where I'd almost been squashed flat by a bus ("you might as well put that boy on a bear as a bike" – Auntie Glad), past a line of derelict shops (haunted) to the traffic lights on Cemetery Road, where you could either go left (to the shops), right (to Hell) or straight on (to the sea): that day we went straight on, down past the library with its enormous spiked gates, *the sharpest spikes in the world*, then along the back lane by the short stay car park and out onto the cycle path at the front. Out across the bay it was thick fog, just like every day. It was as if a grey sheet had been hung up to dry, a dense wall of nothingness. We stopped and looked at it for a while but there wasn't much to see. Such a thing! It was hard to imagine that in just a few days we'd be sailing right into it ("through it" – Mikey). "Do you think there is something across the bay?" I said and Michael said yes, otherwise it wouldn't be a bay. I nodded soberly, though geography wasn't really my strong point. How drab it all was! Looking out across the wet sand was like waiting for the TV to warm up, but it never did. "Shall we go up the Knob?" Mikey said and I said yes and we got back on our bikes and peddled along the front, past the crazy-golf (closed), the amusement arcades (deserted) and the out-doors café (boarded up), and then out along the coast road, leaving our bikes on the gravel beneath Knob Rock, our town's most famous sight, at least for schoolboys. There were crunched up beer-cans and broken glass scattered by the Balls, as well as graffiti that my brother wouldn't let me read, but then the path climbed up amongst the gorse bushes to the electricity substation and the radio transmission tower and a tiny crag where you could look out on the whole bay (our side) and our little seaside town, the houses scattered higgledy-piggledy as if dropped from a great height. "It's funny to think that all this will still be here when our boat's set sail," said my brother. "This crag, the houses, the shops and people – they'll still be here, but we'll be gone." I'd never thought of this before. "Will all my toys be safe?" I asked and he nodded. "And my comics too?" Try as I might I couldn't imagine the little town without me. I mean, what kind of world would it be without me in it? Like a bathtub with the plug pulled out... Our eyes scanned the grey horizon. "Look, is that a seal?" I said and he said, "No, it's a buoy," and I said, "A boy like me?" and he said, "There is no boy like you," but then we started to get a bit hungry so we freewheeled back home.

3

The next night there was an 'extraordinary' town meeting at the community centre, but I was too little to go ("Why would a child want to go anyway? To listen to that flock of geese?" – Granny Dwyn). My dad went, and Uncle Glyn and Uncle Tomos and our neighbours, Mr and Mrs Begham, who didn't have any tickets, but did have a car, which was handy. It didn't sound extraordinary though. There weren't enough seats, the radiators wouldn't work, and nobody from the shipping company remembered to turn up. "I have, however, received a call from head office," said Mr Llewellyn, though, under sustained interrogation, he had to admit that it had been a very bad line and he couldn't be "one hundred percent" sure it was them. After this, questions were invited from the floor. What about those without tickets? When would the boat be returning? How was the selection made in the first place? No one had any answers though – not even Mr Llewellyn and his phone call. When Dad came home he lowered himself down onto our settee as if he was never going to leave it again. "You'd think the ship had sunk!" (Mum). Dad always looked like that though – Uncle Glyn was much jollier. "Quick, quick, outside!" he yelled, coming in the door. "The ship has just sailed into our back garden!" It hadn't though. "Don't pester the boy," said Dad. "He's away with fairies as it is." "Tch, it's just gone," said Uncle Glyn, winking.

We didn't know it at the time, but this wasn't to be the only false alarm. The very next day our local paper published pictures of the "luxury vessel" on its front page, only it turned out to be just a snap of a model, taken in somebody's bath. I stuck it up on my wall anyway. "Do you think we'll have a cabin near the chimneys?" I asked, but my brother wouldn't even look up from his textbook. The boat in the picture was enormous, if you ignored the fact that it fitted in a bathtub. "There must be room for a thousand people," I said, trying to count the portholes, which wasn't easy, particularly on the other side. My brother, ever suspicious, wanted to know why nothing had appeared on the TV or the local news yet, especially if no one had ever crossed the water before. My mother said that of course somebody had been across the water, just not us. "Ask your father!" she snapped. But there was no point. Sorrow sat on my father's head like a large, grey hat. "Why now?" he cried. "Just when I've got all this work on!" My three grannies were worried too. There had been a spate of burglaries since the 'day of the tickets', and they now refused to leave the house. "What if someone goes through my things?" lamented Granny Mair, though I'd been through her things millions of times and never found anything worth stealing. Granny Dwyn slept with a pool-cue under her bed and who could blame her? There were stories of violent break-ins, muggings, aggravated assault. "The whole town is going to the dogs!" (Auntie Glad). According to Dad I was going to the dogs too. As the day crept closer and I got giddier and giddier. "Will it be soon?" I asked my mum, bouncing off the walls. My brother rolled his eyes. "What do you think, Mum? Is the ship sailing towards us even now?" Mum smiled and nodded. Four more sleeps! I looked up at the picture on my wall and made boat noises until everything went black.

All that week there were rumoured sightings of the mysterious cruise-ship. Some kids hanging around by the precinct said that they'd seen an enormous boat of some kind passing the spit of land out by the long-stay car park, though a rival gang contradicted this by claiming they'd spotted a "strange glowing galleon" docking at what had once been an old chemical plant (when no agreement could be reached, fisticuffs broke out). It was as if the mysterious ferry was everywhere. A cloud shaped *exactly* like a paddle steamer passed over the local off-licence. At night, next-door's garage looked like a tug moored amongst the rhododendrons. Even Aunt Bea admitted to dreaming about a luxury liner sailing up the dual carriageway, its "decks ablaze with lanterns". "Shhh," said Uncle Glyn. "That's its whistle blowing out to sea." But where, my brother wanted to know, was such a huge craft going to dock anyway? Our little town had neither harbour nor docks nor jetty. The 'beach' was thick brown mud, sticky as tar (I had once kicked my football in and the mud had swallowed it up like a pill). How would the boat even reach us? But that didn't stop everyone from gazing longingly (or fearfully) at the horizon. Someone even put ten pence in the telescope, though there wasn't much to see: just blobs and squiggles and marks, and beyond that, nothingness. If anything the fog actually seemed a little bit thicker. "Unless it clears, it'll never reach us," said Dad, but that didn't stop Mother from packing her summer dresses.

Then, two days before the date indicated on the tickets, a strange shape appeared out in the bay, like a heavy cloud fallen to earth. Was that smoke coming from a series of smokestacks, or (*mam bach*) just another bank of fog, merely a little heavier than the rest? "Feh, you might as well stare at tea-leaves," said Granny Dwyn, for whom the sky was half-empty, not half-full. No one could even agree as to what shape it was – straight line, oblong, blob. One smart-arse even said it was just a smear on the lens of the telescope, though everyone knew you could see it with your own two eyes, at least if you squinted the right way. Even though the bay was a long way from our house, I couldn't stop myself peeping through the curtains, hoping to catch the boat just waiting outside. "See what you've done," my father grumbled, but Uncle Glyn just grinned and yelled, "Two more days till we walk the plank!" At night I squirmed helplessly in my bed, dreaming of the "glorious dawn" to come, but in the morning the ship stayed stubbornly frozen on the horizon, more of a stain than a ship…

Indeed that morning, as I remember it, everybody seemed a little subdued. All the talk was of travel sickness and vaccinations and injections but the whole room went quiet when I rounded the kitchen table. "What about the sickness…" asked Michael, but Mum said, "Shh – little ears," and eyed me up suspiciously: I'd forgotten to put any trousers on and my hair was sticking out at a funny angle. "The poor dove!" (Auntie Glad). And there was another reason for the pall hanging over our kitchen table: some "wee boy" had drowned out in the bay, seemingly trying to swim out to the phantom ship. The story of his disappearance passed swiftly from house to house, though no one seemed to be able to say where he'd come from, what school he went to, or even how old he was – even his name seemed to have sunk down into the depths. For some reason the story of the boy had a great impact on my family. Granny Dwyn argued that I should be locked in my bedroom "until the whole thing blows over", but after a long argument this was vetoed, two to one. Nevertheless, everyone looked at me strangely. I had a funny glint in my eye and also seemed a little feverish. "You need to keep an eye on that boy," said Aunt Glad. "He looks like a firecracker about to go off." But who wouldn't be a little over-heated? The passenger-ship seemed to be sailing up and down the kitchen, puffs of smoke floating up from its chimneys, forming little speech bubbles as they went.

My worried parents examined me thoroughly: I was "peaky" and "hollow-eyed". There were rumours of people falling ill right across town but people seemed too busy with their packing to pay them much attention. Even when Mr Muller was found dead in his bed, "stiff as an ironing board", all that people talked about was whether he'd received his tickets or not and whether that would mean an extra space, a refund, maybe even some kind of delay? Ah, poor Mr Muller! All anybody could think about was "the other shore", passage across that "deathly span" (Uncle Tomos). But was there really any such thing? The 'ship' itself was still no more than a spill or a mark – as my brother pointed out, it actually looked a little *less* ship-like if anything. Still, fewer and fewer people now seemed to doubt its almost unbearable presence. The less there was to see, the more it seemed to fill people's heads – right up to the brim…

And then, on the very last day, "the dread hand of disaster" (Cousin Alwyn) reached out for our family too. Grandy had been standing atop a footstool, trying to get his suitcase down from his wardrobe, when his famous steamer trunk (it was rumoured to have survived at least one war and maybe two) fell down and brained him. Later on, it turned out that the case was full of pictures of pretty ladies who looked very nice but were, in fact, indecent. Grandpa lay on the floor for a full seven hours before my three grannies found him lying prone and covered in bare bosoms. "Women: the world's sorrow!" The doctor wrapped his head in bandages and confirmed what we all knew: Grandfather wouldn't be able to go. Not even if his head suddenly got better. "I didn't know you *wanted* to go," said Mother and Grandy said, "When did anyone think to ask?" Poor Grandy: even under all those bandages you could tell his brow was furrowed.

We all gathered by his bedside and I accidentally sat on his knee. "With this amount of care, you could kill someone!" But after this we all went quiet: were we going to go on the boat or not? It was "time to poop or get off the pot" (Uncle Glyn). All three grannies, even the one who never said anything, agreed that they were going to stay to look after Grandy. Auntie Glad told everyone that in that case, they weren't going to get her on board that "floating casket" (her words) either. In the end only Mum and Dad and Aunt Bea and Uncle Glyn said they were still going, though my dad said this through gritted teeth (it was hard to tell what my cousins were doing – there were so many of them and they all kept moving around).

But for everybody else though, it was as if a kind of line had been crossed: on the one side was Grandpa's bed, on the other the gangplank leading to the great boat. Tears were shed. Cheeks were kissed. But I wasn't feeling too well either. The room wobbled like it was being cooked in a frying pan. After filling my face with Newbury Fruits I went and threw up in Grandy's hallway. And then it was time to go.

4

By the time we got home, I felt terribly dizzy. My skin crawled and the room swayed from side to side as if I were already onboard ship. Mum put me straight to bed and I lay there sweating and shivering under the covers, all sorts of strange things racing through my head: the suitcase landing on Grandpa's head, Mr Muller stiff as an ironing board, the flickering lanterns of the passenger-ship moored in the bay – it was as if I couldn't make sense of anything. But the main thing I thought about, the thing that stuck in my head more than anything, was the drowned boy. I imagined the water pressing down on his head, his limbs growing heavier and stranger, the seaweed dragging him down to the bottom as it got more and more dark. Ah me, such weight, such darkness! Only Mum pulling the covers back woke me up.

For a second I didn't know which was my blankets and which was the sea – my bed seemed very big and very strong. But even as I kicked and wrestled with my bedding I could hear something telling me I had to get up and go and fetch Dad: our boat was leaving in only a few hours and we all had to make sure we were on board. Buttoning my coat up over my pyjamas I felt heavy and full of sleep. Ah, why couldn't my brother go? He was much bigger and stronger than me. But some shape (Mum?) pulled on my wellies and led me down the stairs – shh, she said, I was a big boy and not to make such fuss. Her hands seemed enormous and she picked me up and carried me over to the door with hardly any effort at all. Such a strange thing! The boat was leaving on the morning tide and we have to be there to meet it. "Mustn't let it leave without us!" Mum (Mum?) wrapped a little red scarf around my neck and kissed the top of my head but it was so dark I couldn't tell whether it was Mam or not. "Mummy, your hands are awful big," I said, but by that point I was out of the door and standing in the street, the bottom of my pyjamas sticking out from under my coat. It was very, very quiet out there: no cars, no passers-by, no cats, no nothing. The only thing I could see was the fog. A sodden bank of mist obscured the streetlights, the houses, even the other side of the road. Our house seemed to exist on a tiny island of solid ground in an enormous sea of grey. It was like somebody had rubbed away at our town with an eraser. "Mummy?" I whispered, but she seemed to have disappeared too.

Outside the fog turned the streetlights into pale, watery circles and everything felt terribly damp: my coat, my scarf, even my pyjamas underneath. Tiny droplets clung to every surface, every inch, little pinpricks of moisture which dribbled down my neck. It seemed impossible to distinguish between the clouds, the fog and the puddles; all was turned into the same murky gloop. If only they had sent my brother Michael instead! After all, he was so much older and smarter than me... But what could I do? Our house had already disappeared into nothingness, replaced by a wall of wet, grey gloom. What a "predicament" (Mikey), what a mess! I mean, what was my dad doing out here in the middle of the night anyway? Was he at the workingmen's club, the leisure centre, the shops? Not knowing what else to do I walked down our road, past the take-away and the post office, all the way into town.

The fog smelt of salt water and petrol, the edge of the shopping area the boundary of the known world. On one side were shops, on the other side the void, "that dark sea into which all things must fall" (Uncle Tomos). Tides without shores, sea without land, nights without end; it was as if the other side had travelled to our little town

24

to meet me… 'Say good-bye to the day,' I thought. 'Give my regards to the dear green earth…' My feet felt awful cold in my wellies. I paddled past a row of empty window-displays and shuttered shops, listening to my boots squelch along the pavement. How lonely it seemed, how silent! It was as if my wellies were the only sound on the planet. In my pocket was a packet of toffees, so I had one. The fog was getting thicker and thicker – or ficker and ficker as Iestyn in our class would say. There seemed only one path through it – a pale luminous corridor, like walking down a pipe. Everything was dripping and I really needed the loo, but where else could I go? No, there was no going back now…

Listen: the path led down past the empty shell of the market, to the very edge of the sea itself. There were no lights anywhere, the windows in the houses little black holes. Dad, Dad, where are you? Was he out at work, away saying goodbye to his chums, at some kind of farewell party? (What would the guests say – "Goodbye, goodbye, goodbye?") Tiny pearls dotted my bright red scarf, each one a perfect little sphere. Ah, if only I'd brought a hat – my hair was plastered to my head. Our little wet town wobbled and dripped, the air soft and damp, like walking through a sponge. Dark shelters dotted the prom, the occasional bench, wet, rusted railings. On the other side of the road there were a number of pubs, known for their rowdiness and violence, but tonight all was peaceful. The fog seemed to take off the sharp edges of the place, blurring all the lines and blotting out the shapes. No taxis, no cars, no nothing. And over the dark wall, the sea itself…

Aside from the wall, all I could see was fog. There was neither up nor down, top or bottom, above or below. It was as if a great grey hood had been placed over my face. Poor me, I thought: how was I supposed to find my daddy in all this soup? I tried to picture Dad in a paper hat, sitting at a round table surrounded by all his electricians, and then I tried to picture where this table might be, and how I might be able to get there, but my thoughts kept getting lost along the way. 'Please help, sir,' I thought, 'I'm only wee.' But I couldn't go home without Dad: what would Mum say, or Michael, or even the people in charge of the boat? No, there was nothing for it: I climbed up onto the wall and tottered unsteadily along the top, holding out my arms like a tightrope walker.

I still felt kind of wobbly though. On one side there was something, on the other side nothing, and it was an awfully fine line between them. But when I say 'nothing', I don't really mean that… no, if you stared deeply into the fog you could make out tiny gaps and hills and mounds, little dark dimples and strange floating lines and shapes. It's true! The more you stared at it, the more detailed it seemed to become, the fog opening up to reveal peaks, craters, valleys, a whole other world – like gazing out onto the landscape of the moon.

And so pretty too, glowing with a tender, lunar light. What a feeling, what light! Walking the wall I felt somehow weightless, as if with a single bound I might float free from our town and spin high above the skyline, a tiny rocket-shaped boy. How big was I? No more than the smallest speck of moon dust, a dot on the picture, a smudge on the lens. And down below me were great sea-less seas, huge bays, lakes, inlets, the toothless mouth of the man in the moon. Ho, I could see him now: the long arched eyebrows, black lipsticked lips, mug that looked like a lopsided birthday cake. He felt awful close – like I could reach out and poke him in the eye! Man in the moon, man in the moon, is that you? Oh, I've seen those donkey eyes of yours before… But then the fog started shifting again and his face faded back into that soft silvery landscape. Goodbye, goodbye, goodbye! In front of me were great grey cliffs, enormous ashen clouds, fogbound caves, beaches, rocks. Was this the opposite shore? Oh Mister Moon, who would have guessed that the other side would prove so close? Yes, I was nearly there: the Sea of Clouds, the Bay of Seething, the Sea of Snakes. Close up the moon looked like an enormous trampoline:

who knew how high you could jump?

And that's when I knew it, knew it like I'd known nothing else in my life. It would take only the tiniest slip – no more than a step really, not even a hop or a skip or a jump – and I would be there too, free from this world, passing soundlessly from one sphere to the next. Ah, who wouldn't be tempted? Who wouldn't pause for a moment, standing there teetering on the very edge of – well, something else?

But even as I hovered on the brink I heard a voice behind me and turned to see a figure emerging from the gloom, no more than a silhouette or a cut-out, but no less familiar for all that. The figure swam through the fog towards me, arms outstretched, legs kicking wildly. My father, the astronaut! But how could I know it was really him? He seemed so close and so big! Then enormous hands grabbed me (just like before!) and the next thing I knew I was back on the earth, his eyes as dark as craters, a huge wet dewberry hanging down from his nose.

"Stupid boy," he growled, "stupid little pup..."

Struggling to get my breath back, I stared hard at his gloomy, careworn mug.

"Why didn't you tell me about the party, Daddy? Mum told me to come and get you but I didn't know where to go."

"Idiot boy..."

Dad's arms felt tremendously solid and I thought: how lucky I am to have a Daddy this big and this strong. Even the fog makes way for him...

"What were you doing up there Alex?" he asked, panting. "Where did you think you were going?"

I tried pointing up at the moon but my arms weren't long enough.

"Why did you go to the party, Daddy? I didn't know where you were..."

Other figures were appearing amongst the fog now, Mikey, some unknown grown-ups, possibly a policeman. I felt wrapped up inside the fog as if inside a soft, wet tissue. There were voices but I couldn't really hear any of them: everything was too muffled and too damp. When I turned my head in one direction there was fog, and when I looked the other way there was more fog too. Ah, who knew how deep it was? It seemed to go on forever, as if that other world were much larger than this one. Such a thing, I thought. Maybe this one is the real world after all…

I looked round for Dad but he was talking to a fella in a funny hat. They were no more than hazy shapes, blurry outlines, shadows in the gloom.

"Mikey?" I said. "Mikey, did you come too?"

The shapes moved and merged and I had the impression of being carried by some irresistible force – maybe Dad, maybe the fella in the funny hat. Strange shapes came and went; it was both our town and not our town, the right things but in the wrong place, everything too big or too small or too broken. It seemed like the town was being carried past me rather than vice versa, the streets some kind of model or display, a carnival float that went on and on and on. The houses rolled by me as if they were on wheels. The sea smelt of glue and balsa wood. Fog clung to everything like an old winter coat.

But then I must have nodded off or something because the next thing I saw was our street and then our garden and then our house and my bedroom and finally Mum herself.

"Mummy, why didn't you send Michael?" I asked. "He's much cleverer than I am and would have known the way for sure…"

Mum's face was very pale, her eyes drawn on with coal.

"Shh," she said, unwrapping my scarf and loosening the buttons on my coat. "You're not well, you've got a fever…"

"I've been across the bay," I said. "It's very nice, Mum, really lovely…"

"Mm…"

"Like sailing to the moon…"

"Hush now," she said, pulling off my boots and wrapping the

bedclothes around me. "It's alright, you're back home now…"

"Home?"

I lay in my bed and let the world rearrange itself around me. There were my toys and over by the cupboard were my board games and there on the chair was floppy dog. Yes, everything was just as it always was. And I felt very safe like that, surrounded by all the things most dear to me. My pictures, my animals, my comics: they'd been there waiting for me all that time. Indeed, it was impossible to imagine being anywhere else.

But then I remembered: tomorrow our boat set sail. Ah, me! My head was throbbing and my arms still felt terribly heavy, as heavy as that drowned boy, as heavy as the bottom of the heaviest ship in the world. What a tired little boy I was – but how was I ever going to get up in the morning? But if I didn't then the ship would set sail without me and I'd be left behind with Grandpa and Auntie Glad and all my old grannies – just imagine that! Ho, what a fool I'd been – bimbling about in the middle of the night just before *the most important day of my life.* Now Michael and my parents and Uncle Glyn and Aunt Bea would all sail away and I'd be as old as Grandpa by the time they came back. No wonder I felt so bereft, so abandoned. Tell me – who wouldn't cry? Who wouldn't weep? My family were sailing away and I lay there anchored to my bed, sealed up in the same little room…

Rubbing my eyes, I turned to stare at the strange whitish glow behind my curtains. How far it seemed to stretch – how strange its light! Was that a fog horn, blowing somewhere out to sea? Or the horn of the boat summoning all its passengers? I tried moving my legs but nothing seemed to work. My eyes started to droop. Slowly, inexorably, the glow started to fade. The light disappeared, and then the fog, and then the window disappeared too. It was very dark and very quiet. Then there was nothing, not even the dot of an 'i'…

The Sea of Vapours

1

When I woke up, my blanket was green and the walls were beige. All I could see through the porthole was a heavy curtain of grey: sky, fog, sea – who knew? My tiny room rocked and swayed. Engines hummed. Bells rang. 'Ah,' I thought; 'my little bed's set sail after all!' Everything about the room seemed *tremendously* strange. Was the ship just like the one in the picture? Or was it something else entirely? 'The boy stood on the burning deck/the ship was sinking fast/and as he stood there sinking too/the captain floated past...' I wanted to go see, but my legs seemed cut out from paper. Poor Alex! I was a small boy in a small room. My bed was made up on crates. There were boxes everywhere. When I looked up, the porthole was round and grey, like a big blind eye. Then, when I looked back down, an enormously hairy man was staring right at me, his whiskers perilously close to my face. And such whiskers! Like some kind of bear that had been stuffed into a long white coat.

"Hello my lad," he said. "Back in the land of the living are we?"

"I don't know sir."

"Ha ha. Well, we'll soon see. My name is Dr Beedie. Can you say that?"

"Birdie?"

"Beedie."

"Beenie?"

"Close enough. So how are you feeling my lad?"

"A bit tired sir."

"Mmm. Can you lift your right arm up for me?"

"Yes sir."

"Mm. And your other right arm? That's it. And do you still have all your legs?"

"I've got two, sir."

"Just enough! As long as they reach the ground, eh? Now, open your pyjamas and let me have a listen to your chest."

The doctor's jacket was very white and his stethoscope very cold. But I was more worried about his beard: if I got lost in there then nobody would find me for days. What a pelt, what a fleece! 'Hairy as a hearthrug' as Granny Dwyn would say of Cousin Nona's arms.

"Good … good. Lungs like those will conquer the world. Eh, my boy? You'll be back on your feet in no time."

"Yes sir."

"A strong little fellow, eh?"

"Yes sir."

His voice was very soothing but I couldn't get over how woolly he was. His hands looked like enormous black paws.

"Are we at sea, sir?"

"That's right, lad. All at sea! Now, be a brave boy and open wide."

"What do you want me to open, sir?"

"First your ears and then your mouth. That's it! Lovely lad…"

The fella popped in a thermometer and told me not to bite on it because if it broke I'd be dead in seconds.

"That's it! Hm, and a clever boy to boot…"

Bits of his lunch (Ham? Bacon? Sausage?) were caught up in his whiskers and I remember thinking, poor me, I hope he doesn't eat little boys too…

"Yes, that's fine," he said, shaking the tube in front of my nose. "Not too hot and not too cold! No, this one's just right!"

I couldn't take my eyes off those big white teeth. How many there were and how sharp! They were spread out in a tremendously wide smile.

"Well, my handsome lad, there's plenty more miles in you yet. Just don't go jumping off the side!"

"Yes sir."

"Do you feel hungry?"

"Yes sir."

"Do you feel thirsty?"

"Yes sir."

"Do you need to go pee?"

"I already have sir."

"Just so. I'll go and tell your parents."

And with that the fella was gone.

The next thing I knew a suit walked into the room with my father inside. How tidy he looked! Hair brushed back, tie straight, chin smooth. He looked awful tired though. He looked me up and down as if I were a very heavy weight he'd had to carry a very long way.

"So how are you feeling, my lad?"

"M'okay."

"Sure?"

"Yes sir."

Dad rubbed his eyes thoughtfully and then spread his hands out wide on the bed.

"Not too cold?

"No…"

"Not too hot?"

"No sir."

He nodded. Somewhere a bell sounded and we listened to it for a while. How doleful it sounded! As dismal as the view through the porthole. Dad's suit sat awkwardly on my bed and I pulled myself up to look at him.

"Alex? What were you doing out on that sea-wall?" he said.

I grinned. "I was looking for you, Daddy. Mum told me to go out and fetch you."

"Mm," he said, patting the top of my head. His hands seemed surprisingly clean.

"Was the party nice, Dad? Did you have cake?"

"There was no party Alex…"

"But if there was no party then why did Mum send me out to get you?"

"You're getting everything mixed up Alex. You weren't well, you had some kind of fever…"

Dad was looking at me like you'd look at a sick horse: "one eye on the fetlocks, the other on the gun" (Cousin Gethin).

"Dad? Did you carry me to the boat?"

"You were very sick. We had to wrap you up in a blanket."

I thought about this for a while. My pyjamas were very prickly.

"What was it like when we went down to the boat? Were there lots of people waving and cheering?"

"No Alex."

"Was there a band?"

"There wasn't a band. It was very early. It was still dark."

I looked across and saw that my floppy dog was there, and my suitcase and two pairs of shoes: one brown and one black. I didn't know if Mum had packed my stickers or my soldiers though.

"Is it a big ship Daddy?"

"Big enough for a boy like you…"

"Is it higher than our house?"

"Yes, Alex."

"Is it a hundred miles long?"

"No, Alex."

"Is there room for everybody in the world and then a friend?"

"Time to get some rest Alex. You're still not well."

My father, the doctor!

When Mum came in she was dressed in a pretty blue dress and smelt vaguely of vanilla. She put her hand on my forehead and brushed back my hair. Her hand was very cool and made me think of ice cream.

"How are you feeling?"

"A bit hot. Have I got cabin fever?"

Mum re-arranged the covers and stroked my cheek.

'I don't think so. Do you want anything to eat?"

"Do they have ice cream?"

"Oh, they've got everything…"

Mum smiled but her eyes seemed strangely distant and I wondered if she'd been reading her Russian books again.

"Have you been out?" I asked.

"Out?"

"Out on top, I mean."

"On the deck?"

"Mm."

Mum's nails were really short and really blue: when she bit them did she end up with blue teeth too?

"Yes, I've been out on the deck."

"What does the sea look like Mummy?"

"Like the sky, only wetter."

I nodded.

"Mum?"

"Mm?"

"Mum? Why did you send me?"

"Send you?"

"To get Dad I mean. Michael is so much smarter than I am…"

Mum looked wistful and pushed some hairs down on to the top of my head.

"Oh Alex… I didn't send you Alex. You were dreaming, you weren't well…"

"It was very far…"

"Shh – we all have to be in the dining room at seven, and big boys need their sleep…"

"But…"

"You're still not well Alex, you need to rest…"

"But I want to come. I won't make a mess – my hands are really very big. I don't like this room Mummy, can I come?"

Mum pulled a face and looked tired.

"There'll be another night Alex. You have to wait till you feel a bit better. You understand don't you? That's it. There's a big brave boy…"

"I…"

"Shh then."

I was about to ask her something else but just at that moment somebody shouted "knock knock" and the next thing I knew Aunt Bea and Uncle Glyn appeared as if they'd been pulled out of a hat.

"Hello, hello," beamed Uncle Glyn. "How's my favourite midget?"

"Shh," said Aunt Bea. "Your uncle's just being silly. Now let me take a look at you…"

Bea brushed my hair exactly like Mum had only a few minutes before. Where was Mum anyway? Aunt Bea's lips were very red.

"How are you feeling Alex?"

I shrugged.

"Pfft!" said Uncle Glyn. "Why ask the chicken about the soup?

Just look at him – the boy is fine. C'mon Alex, it's dinnertime in a minute. Don't want to miss dessert!"

I tried to get up but it was like somebody had cut my strings. How weak I was – "Feeble as a kitten's kick!" (Grandy).

"Are you okay, Alex?" asked Aunt Bea.

"A little tired, maybe…"

"Too tired to eat?"

"Can you save me something, Uncle Glyn? Pop something in your pocket for me…"

Uncle Glyn was also dressed in his best bib and tucker, hair slicked back, gut pulled in. He looked less tired than Dad though, or maybe better ironed.

"No need for that, boy. Just ring your bell and they'll bring you whatever you want."

"Even ice cream?"

"Buckets of it!"

"Shh, let him rest," said Aunt Bea, her beautiful red lips floating in front of her face. "Plenty of time for ice cream later…"

"I won't miss it, will I?" I asked. "The boat, I mean…"

Aunt Bea smiled. "No, Alex, you won't miss a thing…"

"What's it like? Is it big?"

"The boat? Well, the staff are awful attentive…"

"Does it have chimneys?"

"Chimneys?"

"Three big chimneys with smoke. Like in the picture!"

"Mm," said Aunt Bea, "I suppose so." Her eyes sparkled suggestively. "And there's dancing every night. A ballroom and observation deck and everything…"

Aunt Bea was awful similar to my mother, though her dress was a different colour. I looked around for Mum but I couldn't see her anywhere.

"Can I go dancing with you, Aunt Bea?"

"Shh – you need to get your strength back first. Do what the doctors tell you, okay Alex?"

I nodded sadly.

"And drink your medicine straight down…"

"Yes sir."

Her lips floated back to her face and she gave me a tremendous wink.

"That's a good boy. We all have to go now 'cause it's dinnertime but … you tell the doctor if you need anything, okay Alex?"

"Yes sir."

Aunt Bea looked concerned.

"Are you sure you're going to be okay Alex?"

"Yes sir."

"There's a good lad," said Uncle Glyn, springs groaning as he struggled to his feet. "No tossing on the high seas…"

I watched them go and thought, 'My beautiful aunt and jolly uncle – how big they seem!' The space seemed awful empty without them.

After that my cabin was quiet for a while. There wasn't much to do. I couldn't see anything out of the porthole: it was like it had been sealed up with quick-drying cement. How long would it take us to reach the other side anyway? By the time I was well enough to leave my cabin the whole thing might be over…

I fumbled around for some kind of buzzer or bell but couldn't find anything. My brown floppy dog was there, but just out of reach. With nothing else to do I turned over and went to sleep. The boat was gently rocking from side to side. The blanket felt awful prickly – a bit like my pyjamas. The boat cut through the fog like a knife.

The next time I woke up it was pitch black. The sea was lurching a little more dramatically and my dog had fallen on the floor. Somewhere I could hear music, but I couldn't work out where it was coming from: out on deck maybe, or perhaps in some great ballroom, with streamers and balloons and lights. The music was very pretty but seemed terribly far away, like something playing half way 'cross the world. Ah, how lonely I felt! Violins were playing, people were having fun, and here I was "laid out like a pastry dish" (Uncle Tomos). Then the door opened a little and a skinny figure slipped in through the crack; luckily it was my brother Michael, dressed in shirt and tie, hair stuck down to his hot head.

"Alex? Alex, are you awake?"

"Mm," I said. I didn't know how much time had gone by since Aunt Bea and Uncle Glyn had gone – maybe minutes, maybe years. Michael still looked much the same though.

"I've brought you a chicken leg," he said, handing me a greasy napkin.

"I'm very hungry," I said, taking a bite of chicken and napkin combined.

"How are you feeling Alex?"

Michael had been eating something spicy. Had he had a gulp of wine too? My brother the grown-up!

"A bitty better. Did you bring any ice cream?"

"Now how would I carry that? Here, I stole a chocolate mint. It's a bit squashed…"

"Mikey? What's it like out on deck? Can you see anything? Can you see the other side yet?"

Michael shook his head. "It's very grey. There's fog everywhere. We seem to be going very slow."

I sighed, just like my father. "I haven't even seen the boat…"

"It's not a boat, it's a ship…"

"They're the same thing."

"No they're not. A ship is much bigger."

I tried thinking about this for a while but I was much too tired.

"Mikey? Where did you go? Was it pretty? Did you hear the music?"

Michael sighed. "We've just had dinner. Mum and Aunt Bea are still dancing. I'm going to go to bed now."

"Mikey?"

"Mm?"

"Mikey?"

"What is it Alex?" Mikey was standing by the door now and sounding a little cross.

"Do you think there is another side? Maybe Granny Dwyn was right. Maybe there's nothing across the bay at all."

"Don't be silly Alex. There's another side to everything. Look, you've got sauce all over your pillow…"

"But…"

"Shh – it's very late and you should be asleep. That's it, let go of the chicken leg…"

My clever brother! When he left and switched the light off, my cabin seemed darker than ever. The boat – ship! – swayed gently and I felt as if I was at the bottom of some enormous black hole. I meant to ask Mikey how deep the sea was, but I forgot. It certainly felt a long way down to me.

2

It was another couple of days before I was finally allowed out. Michael was right: out on deck it was very, very grey. The sea like slate, the sky leaden, the mist the colour of concrete. Above me, strange gulls followed the ship, swooping and squawking and covering everything in shit. How terrifying they were! Bethan said that if you carried a sandwich out on deck, they'd strip you to the bone in seconds: I didn't believe her but still, I kept my soft, pink fingers in my pockets – just in case.

Bethan was a girl around my age who had taken to hanging around with Aunt Bea and Uncle Glyn. Aunt Bea and Uncle Glyn didn't have any children of their own but attracted other people's kids like "wasps to a jam pot" (Granny Mair). Bethan was "smaller than a gnat's hankie" (Uncle Glyn), but had a tough, scrunched-up little face, like a boxer on the ropes. She was a scrapper, a biter and a scratcher. But what a gal! We played 'bomb' and 'stink' and took turns trying to wee on passers-by from the lifeboats. "Alex," she'd call, her voice like honey, "Alex, come and play..."

Whilst I hung around with Bethan, Michael played chess with Dr Kutchner from C Deck, an old fella with a long red nose who spoke *exactly* like a villain from an old war film. "With this game, you have made ... von mistake," he would hiss, watching my brother move his prawns ("pawns!" – Michael) across the board. "Yes, yes: that too is an error. Let me see if you can see how to escape. No – no, you do not!" Mikey wouldn't let me play because I made neighing noises whenever I picked up the horsey, but I liked watching the two of them moving their little chunks of wood across the squares, making funny little patterns with their rooks and bishops and whatnot. Sometimes I would whisper in Michael's ear, "Attack him with your king," and Dr Kutchner would say, "Your brother: he is a little *einfach*, yes?" and Michael would nod and pat me sadly on my head.

If I had Bethan, and Michael had Dr Kutchner, then Aunt Bea had Able Seaman Able. Able Seaman Able wore a very impressive White Star uniform and had a magnificently large, high-peaked hat. Uncle Glyn said that he was the kind of fellow "too busy polishing his teeth to wipe out his poop deck" but Aunt Bea found him "*trés gallant*", and admired the cut of his jib. Uncle Glyn rolled his eyes in despair. "This ship is awash with seamen!" The most striking things about Able Seaman Able were his eyes (two) which he used to stare dramatically out at the fog. I tried asking him about the opposite shore and what would happen when he got there, but he just shook his head and squinted into the middle distance, "his cold blue eyes fixed on eternity" (Uncle Tomos). He was "imperturbable" (Michael). In fact, apart from the terrifyingly hairy doctor, most of the White Star crew seemed pretty tight-lipped. "It's because they're *professional*" (Mother). I had my doubts though; I mean, what if they turned out to be different from us, even (shh, whisper it softly!) from *the other shore*? I tried spying on the woman who came in to empty my bin but she saw me hiding behind the door and I had to pretend to be playing hide and seek instead.

Otherwise life onboard ship was just the same as life back home. I mean, there was Mr Bellamy from the greengrocers, and Mrs Allen who lived next door to Thomas Truffle's parents, and Mr Chattarji, the dentist. At times it seemed like the whole little town had drowned, the survivors scooped up and placed in one enormous tub. There were still people missing though: no kids from my class, nobody from 'Cooking Club', not even anybody else from down our road.

"Why us and not them?" complained Father, who hated mess and confusion, especially in his locker space. Every day he would march around the decks as if taking a head-count. "Where are you going?" yelled Uncle Glyn, but Father refused to turn back. "When a shark stops moving it's because it's dead!" We watched Dad tramp the whole length of B Deck, a tall, awkward figure, attacked by gulls. "Bea, I married a fool," lamented my mother, watching the birds scream and dive.

Whilst Dad walked the long walk and Mum read about Russians, I was left more or less alone. For some reason I was still quartered in the same cabin I had woken up in, though whether my room was some kind of medical bay or just a spare cubbyhole I couldn't really tell; there were lots of crates and boxes lying around, but also a bed, a night light and a chest of drawers. The door was left unlocked which meant I could wander up and down the ship as I pleased – along the corridors, the galleys, decks. Bethan and I went everywhere together; in and out of the kitchens, through the stuff in the supply hold, round and round the machinery in the propeller room. Occasionally stewards would try to chase us away with their magnificent moustaches but we didn't let that worry us: "life was a dream", as Aunt Bea liked to say. My favourite hidey-hole was at the bottom of the chimneys, breathing in all the fumes and the gas and the crap, but Bethan preferred filling her face in the galley, chocolate in her pockets and custard in her hair… Afterwards we'd play 'I Dare You', Bethan's favourite game. My dares tended to be pretty tame, like eating the last roll at breakfast or throwing things at the boom, but Bethan's were always terrifying; shinning up an observation mast, hanging over the side by one leg, chasing the seagulls with sticks. The one I remember best though was the one about the funnel. Mm, I can see it now: its weird lips, long dark hole, the eerie space beyond…

The funnel was on E Deck, just past the ping pong tables and the purple recliners, about four foot high with a spout as wide as a child. Of course, there were funnels and shafts of all kinds all over the ship – air vents, laundry chutes, ventilation pipes, that sort of thing – but there was something different about this one, something that made us stop playing 'Murder' and stare at it "agog".

"I dare you," Bethan said. "I dare you to slide down inside…"

I looked at Bethan and looked at the hole. Did Bethan say the words or did I just think them?

"I don't know," I said. "It's very small and very dark…"

"I dare you…" said Bethan, her dark eyes flashing. You could see by her little pursed face that she was starting to get angry; besides, her fists were starting to clench and she was rocking from side to side.

"But…"

Her breath came in hot little puffs. "I dare you…" she hissed. At that moment both Bethan and the hole seemed indeterminably terrifying. Which to choose?

"It looks very tight, Bethan, I don't think it goes anywhere…"

Bethan looked at me like a hammer might look at a nail. Her cheeks were very red. There was froth at the side of her mouth.

"I dare *you*…"

I didn't know what to say. Bethan's whole body was rigid as a totem-pole, her face a tight little mask of rage.

"Bethan? Bethan, I…"

Then, before I knew what was going on, the funnel reached out and swallowed me whole. It's true! I heard a tremendous bang as I hit the sides (like the slides at the leisure centre only much, much worse) and then it felt like I was falling through a great black hoop, or maybe a whole series of black hoops, each one darker and tighter than the last. Luckily there was only one place to go though: the bottom, the end, the belly of the beast! I hit the bottom and found myself in a tight metal box full of nothing. No sky, no funnel, no Bethan. I couldn't even see myself.

"Bethan?"

I could feel something hot and hard panting at my back but I wasn't sure what it was – a little girl or some kind of beast? The space felt very cramped and very dark – "dark as the inside of a dog" (Uncle Glyn). It was also awfully smelly – like Dad's overalls, only worse ("if you don't wash those clothes they'll go off to town without you" – Mum). On my back I could feel ten little fingers and ten little nails, but I didn't dare turn round.

"Bethan? I have to go back now. My trousers are dirty and my head is sore…"

But where should I go, up? The shaft was too high and the space was far too tight. What kind of place was this for a little boy? I squeezed past some kind of valve or fitting and then clambered into a second shaft, this one even darker and narrower than the first.

"Bethan, I don't like it here," I whispered. "Bethan?"

I couldn't see her, but I could feel two little arms pushing into my body and ten mean little nails cutting into my skin. Reluctantly I shoved myself forward, crawling along the chute on my front. Sure, it was kind-of dirty, but what could I do? "An army marches on its belly!" (Grandy). And all the time Bethan (Bethan?) was just behind me, her breath practically in my ear.

"Bethan? Not so hard…"

Poor me; crawling along the pipe was like squeezing toothpaste through a tube. Where was I anyway – "the black hole of Calcutta?" (Mum)? The space was smaller than I was. The only good thing was that there wasn't room to be scared: where would you go? In the tum and out the bum! I manoeuvred myself around some kind of junction or bend and the next thing I knew I was squashed in some kind of storage space or glory hole, covered in filth "from stern to bow" (Mikey). There wasn't much to it though: bits of old rope, some old paint cans, piles of plastic tubing. I scrabbled around half-heartedly but the ceiling seemed terribly low: "lower than a dachshund's balls!"

(Cousin Gareth). I could still hear engine noises and a kind of low hum, but didn't have a clue where it was coming from: was there a downstairs on a ship? It all seemed very strange. Bethan was nowhere to be seen and neither was I. Ah, poor Alex! What if the lights came back on and I wasn't even there?

"Bethan?" I whispered. "Bethan, can you hear me?"

Nothing.

"Bethan, are you there?"

Heavy breathing.

"Bethan? I'm going now. Okay Bethan?"

I followed the shaft a little way, pretending the pipes were worms and the shaft a long dark tunnel. It was still pretty narrow – "tighter than a mouse's corset!" (Uncle Glyn) – but at least it seemed to lead somewhere: "better someplace than no place" as Granny Mair said at the crematorium.

At the end of the shaft I came across a hatch and some kind of frosted glass partition blocking the way through. I tried craning my neck, but it wasn't easy to see: behind the partition was what seemed like a very long dormitory or maybe some sort of sick room – some place with lots of beds in it anyway. Either way, there were lots of grown-ups in pyjamas inside, milling around the beds or lying down on top of them, and the beds seemed to go on and on and on. The patients (patients?) didn't look so good though: some sat propped up at a long table playing cards, whilst others read books or just lay there, limp and exhausted, like empty sacks. Even the younger ones looked kind of peaky – wrinkly somehow, as if in need of a good iron. What were they all doing lying here at the bottom? Shouldn't they be out playing ping pong, taking the vapours, breathing in all that healthy sea air? I breathed hard on the glass, wiped it with my sleeve, and that's when I saw him: Grandy, *our* Grandy, propped up like a cushion, his bald head shining. I couldn't believe it, "not even if I polished my eyes with spit!" (Uncle Glyn). 'Grandy/ Grandy/

old and lean!/Short of patience/and long of spleen.' Little mother, dear heart! But what was he doing here and not "safe and sound" on dry land? Wasn't he too sick, too poorly to leave his bed? Not that he looked all that "full of beans" now, to be honest. I mean, he just lay there, slumped over a table, and moving his arms in a very odd way. And wasn't that Auntie Glad just across from him, laid out on her bed like a picture in a frame? It was, it was! Auntie Glad, Auntie Glad – it's me, Alex, your special little man! But what was everybody doing here? Waiting for something? Waiting for me? I was about to bang on the door when I felt a blast of hot air on my neck.

"Bethan?"

When I turned round, a great hairy face was staring straight at me, a long pink tongue sticking out of the fuzz like a root.

"Sir?"

The doctor smiled benignly and patted me gently on the head.

"Why, my lovely boy! So how are you feeling these days my lad? Any stronger?"

"I'm a lot better sir," I said, looking up at him. "My legs are still working, and my lungs too."

"There's a good boy. And your brother Michael, he's well too?"

"Yes sir. He's even bigger than I am."

"Just so. Right then my boy, let's head back upstairs, shall we? What you need to feel now is the wind on your cheeks."

I wanted to ask him about Grandy but didn't quite dare. Maybe it hadn't been Grandy at all: I mean, what with the frosted glass and all, it had been kind-of hard to see. Maybe it was just some other old fella or a picture of him – a cut-out, like the picture of the ship. In Grandy's house there was a picture of Grandy on his wedding day and he wasn't even in it.

Either way, it was all too late now. We walked back through various doors and hatches and eventually reached a much larger (and better-lit) staircase. I couldn't take my eyes off Dr Beedle though. His tongue flicked out from that thick mass of hair. It was very, very pink.

"So, young fellow, how are you finding the trip? Everything just as you imagined?"

"The boat's very big. Is there room for everyone we know and then a friend?"

"Oh, at the very least. And the food? To your liking?"

"Yes sir. I like chips."

"Yes," he said, looking at me. "You seem a little more ... plump. Now you run along, handsome boy. I'll be seeing you soon enough."

The top of the stairs opened out onto the first deck, and immediately I could smell the sea, the chimneys, lunch.

"Goodbye Dr Boney," I said, skipping away.

"Goodbye lad. Stay well."

Waving goodbye, the doctor licked his lips and went back to his cave. Goodbye Dr Boney, Goodbye!

When I opened the door, Bethan was waiting for me. Her face was red and she was rocking from side to side like a tiger ready to pounce.

"I dare *you*..." she hissed.

3

I decided not to tell my mum and dad about Grandy: what to tell? Besides, Mum and Dad weren't getting on. First one, the the other, would take turn standing outside their cabin, gazing out mournfully at the great blank sea. Father was worried about the tickets: there was something funny about them, something about the way they were stamped. Other people worried about Father – "I've seen healthier looking people in the grave!" (Uncle Glyn). Of course it might just have been the sickness: the water had got a bit choppier now, and the boat ("ship!") went up and down like Father's lunch. Mum too seemed "preoccupied" (Mikey), her pale eyes pensive and sad. "Your mother's got an artistic temper" (Aunt Bea). "So, who took away her brushes?" (Uncle Glyn). What was she looking for anyway, out there on the horizon, drifting amongst the waves and the fog? It wasn't as if there was anything to see out there: the water stretched out like a blanket and the sky was the colour of glue. "Is she in Russia again?" I'd ask and Michael would look at me and nod. My sad mummy! It was like she was far from us, even though she was right there on the deck. Other times she'd put on something bright and clingy and go dancing with Aunt Bea. Mikey and Father didn't like this either. "One tap scalding, the other cold!" (Dad). It was like I had two mothers, one the sun, the other the moon. 'My Mel-an-choly Momma/Where you been all sum-mer?' Sometimes I'd sit at her side and follow her eyes as they moved slowly across her book, wander off across the deck, and fly away into the fog and beyond… But what could you do? Everything smelt salty, and if you sat out on deck, you smelt salty too. Back in my cabin I'd secretly sniff my knees, the smell making me think of crisps – or scampi maybe. My hair would be very wet: my eyebrows also. "Where have you been?" asked Uncle Glyn. "Washing barnacles off the bottom?" In the morning I'd find little bits of salt in my tummy button, stuck to my arms, even in the corner of my eyes.

I still went playing with Bethan, but more and more doors seemed locked now, whole sections "out of bounds". The whole of E Deck seemed to be permanently closed, the way there blocked by cleaners and mops and buckets. Even Dad's daily "peregrinations" (Dad) had had to be curtailed: hatches were closed, corridors locked up, viewing platforms restricted to staff alone. Only one, solitary, lookout remained, from where the two of us would gaze out into the great expanse of nothing we somehow found ourselves floating away in.

"Dad, when will we get there?" I'd ask, and he'd say, "I don't know, son. Not long now."

"It seems an awful long way across the bay."

"Mm."

"I've only got two more pairs of pants."

"Mm."

Dad's face was very creased, like a handkerchief that had been kept in a pocket for far too long. Had Dad seen Grandy on one of his endless "tours"? I didn't dare ask him. Dad looked pale and drawn and climbed down the metal stairwell like an old man. Was he this old when we set out? I watched him trying to swing his legs onto the next rung but then the seagulls attacked us and we had to go back down. "It's just the sickness," said Uncle Glyn. "He'll be right as rain in a day or two." At dinnertime, Uncle Glyn piled his plate so high you couldn't even see him. "All you can eat is an offer not a challenge," complained Aunt Bea, but who could blame him? The food was really, really good. After lunch I'd lay in a sun-lounger and listen to my insides bubble and fizz. And dinner was even better! Chips, pasties, fritters – I could feel the fat being pushed into my fingers like water filling up a glove. Mum and Aunt Bea refused to eat too much 'cause they wanted to go dancing and Dad could barely touch a crumb but Uncle Glyn, Michael and I – ah, we all filled our faces and then some! It didn't matter if the sea went up and down or waves were crashing against the sides – we could always pull up a chair for more.

Dinner was a proper, sit-down affair, with shiny cutlery, starched white napkins and big-stemmed glasses, all set out on long tables in the ballroom. Big burly stewards, their moustaches freshly laundered, served us great mountains of grub, rushing around with huge platters in the crook of their arms. No matter how the ship tossed or swayed, not a single plate was dropped, nor drop of wine spilled, their uniforms as crisp as our napkins. Even so, there was something about them I did not like: when they swooped around our table they reminded me of the seagulls from the top deck, their arms flapping and their eyes terribly cruel. "Wonderful service!" said Mrs Mirozek, and Mr Mirozek nodded and licked the end of his spoon.

Yes, it was quite a spread, all in all: candlelight, gleaming plates, fancy-pants place settings. Every night the captain came and sat at a different table: "every trip a different port". The captain had enormous mutton chops, like two white chickens stuck to his cheeks, and huge bushy eyebrows that seemed to be there to provide cover for his eyes. But the strangest thing about him was his huge soft hat, which was exactly the shape of the ship – I mean with the chimneys and the observation mast and everything. Such a thing! I'd never seen a grown-up wear anything so strange. I kept nudging my brother Michael and pointing but he just shushed me and kicked my shins under the table.

Needless to say everyone around the table wanted to know the same things: how long it would take to cross the bay, would the fog ever clear, when would we finally reach land? Ach, you might as well have asked the ship's cat! All the captain's answers were hidden by coughs and mutters, especially when Dad asked why the tickets were only one way. The only time he really became animated was when the food was served. "Marvellous chicken, eh, very tender," he muttered, his dark eyes gleaming. I watched him intently, and the more I looked at him, the more he started to look like Doctor Beedle, only Dr Beedle after some kind of shave. I thought about it for a while and then accidentally pushed a pea up my nose. "Your son, Alex," asked Mrs Mirozek. "Is he … special?"

At our table there was the captain, Mum and Dad, Mikey, Aunt Bea and Uncle Glyn, the Mirozeks, Mrs Mook from the library and her daughter, Mabel, who was about Mikey's age and tall and skinny as a flagpole. Bethan was sitting with her parents a couple of tables along, kitted out in a little pink dress and looking "as if butter wouldn't melt in her mouth" (Granny Mair). When she saw me she opened her jaws to show me what she'd been chewing and I did the same. "Grrww," I said, drooling a little.

Mrs Mook was trying to ask the captain about postcards: would it be possible to post them when we reached the other side? The captain nodded and opened his mouth as wide as a crocodile. "Oh, oh, no reason to have any worries on that account," he said, mopping up his plate with a slice of crusty bread. "The service is very regular…"

"It's just that I've never heard of anyone receiving mail from across the sea…"

"Tsk, write away my dear! You can be sure that all the people you've left behind will be wondering what has happened to you…"

Postcards were on sale from the ship's kiosk, all of them with pictures of the White Star liner on them: none of them seemed to have pictures of the other shore though – who knew why? Michael then launched into a very long and very technical question about the amount of fuel required for the journey and the size of the ship's engines and all the time Mabel, Mrs Mook's daughter, was drinking him in like a tall glass of milk. Ah, what a funny girl! She was terribly awkward and kept her head bowed at all times. Her hair was done up as if she were still a little girl but she also wore a huge amount of make-up, seemingly applied in the dark. "But what about the maximal co-efficient?" asked Michael, and all the time the girl's head was bobbing like a sunflower.

I tried following what everybody was saying but I soon got distracted. For some reason my plate seemed to want to float up from its setting and drift toward the ceiling, almost as if the whole boat ("ship!") had been turned upside down. Only by closing my eyes could I keep it in its place – and not just my plate but the cutlery and the condiments too. It's true! The captain's mutton chops, Aunt Bea's dress, my special beaker: all of them felt like they were being lifted upwards, pulled on invisible strings. I scrunched up my eyes and concentrated hard. If I opened my eyes at the wrong moment the whole table might fly off! "Are we keeping you up?" asked Dad, nudging me with his elbow.

Just then the ship's band, dressed, like the stewards, in white jackets and white stars, started to play and couples began to edge toward the dance floor, some of them practically floating up from their seats. "So," said Mum, "those feet of yours still planted in the ground?" Dad looked kind-of "green around the gills" so Mum and Aunt Bea led the captain to the floor instead, his hat rising and their dresses billowing. Oh my pretty mother and pretty aunt! One wore black and the other pink ("coral!"), but each looked like a photograph of the other.

"Anyway," said Uncle Glyn, finishing off Dad's pud. "How's that bike of yours these days – still in bits in your kitchen?" And all the time Mum (or was it Aunt Bea) and the captain were dancing real close – like "two feet in one sock" (Granny Dwyn). The coloured lights made it look like it was snowing, but snowing up rather than down. It was all very odd. My napkin fluttered like a bird. The glass next to me shook like it wanted to take off. When I looked across at Mabel, her hair was bobbing above her head like handlebars, while over by the bar, the tables danced as if on wires.

It was only then I noticed that the captain wasn't dancing but was talking to some moustachioed steward off to one side of the band. I wasn't close enough to catch what they were saying, but both looked grim-faced, their mugs the colour of porridge. The captain said something, the steward nodded, and then the pair of them slipped casually away, the captain pulling his strange hat down around his ears. 'T. Rubble,' I thought: 'this spells trouble!' Whilst Dad and Glyn talked carburettors and Mabel stared at Mikey I quickly followed the captain and the steward, floating up the stairs after them like a toy balloon…

I followed the pair of them through the hatch and down the corridor, but as soon as we reached the upper deck, all thoughts of pursuit inexplicably vanished from my brain. I couldn't help it! The fog had vanished and our ship now seemed to be floating in an endless sea of winking lights, a great swathe of stars, stretching as far as the eye could see. Little mother, what a thing! The stars dripped like drops of milk, great swirls and clusters of them, stirred in amongst the blackness. Such beauty, such shapes! And who would have guessed the sky could be so *light*? There were stars everywhere, spilt across the heavens or dotted in the black sea below, luminous streaks and spirals, a great radiant spray of white. And so many dots! Tiny drops of white, each glowing with a soft, kindly light.

Ah, how amazing it was! The stars in the heavens and our ship amongst them – I gazed up at the dribbles and spurts and drank it all in: no plough, no bear, no dipper, just this great milky spray, like cream on the fur of a big black cat. Who could measure it? There were as many stars in the sea as up above me, and no straight line between the two. 'All that milk,' I thought. 'And no one here to drink it!' The more I thought about it, the more light-headed I felt:

all the milk in heaven! Knocked off my feet, I stumbled backwards and ran to go find Mum and Dad. My head was bursting and my breath came in short, sharp bursts. I had to find them *now*!

When I got back to the ballroom it looked like it was just about ready to take off. "Mum, come and see!" I yelled. But it wasn't Mum: it was Aunt Bea dancing with Able Seaman Able, his hairy mitt – quite extraordinarily hairy, in fact – resting on her shoulder like a glove.

"Bea!"

She blinked her eyes and patted me on the head but didn't really seem to hear me.

"Alex?"

"Aunt Bea, Aunt Bea, you've got to come right now!"

She looked at me as my mother might, if I'd come into her room at night, complaining of a bad dream.

"Bea! Bea!"

My beautiful young aunt: but why wasn't she listening to me? "Please!" I begged. "Please Aunt Bea … you've got to come…"

"Alex?"

"You've got to come and see…"

Her dance-partner gestured chivalrously (how hairy his hands were – like two furry tarantulas!) and I pushed past him and started pulling her madly towards the stairs.

"Aunt Bea, Aunt Bea, you won't believe it…"

We pushed our way through the dancing couples and squeezed between the remaining dinner tables, Aunt Bea tottering on her heels.

"Aunt Bea, it's beautiful!"

We climbed up the stairs and raced along the corridor, but by the time we got out onto the deck, the fog had blown back over the sky and only a tiny circle remained, a kind of mirror or little black pool, its surface dotted with lights.

"Look, Bea – stars!"

My beautiful young aunt stared up at them and paused.

"Can you see them? There, look! Stars!"

Aunt Bea laughed and clapped her hands.

"Bea?"

"They're beautiful Alex, really beautiful."

"Do you see them?"

"I see them!"

Her voice sounded funny and I thought, 'Ah, how like mummy she is…'

"Look Aunt Bea! Look how many there are!"

The fog rolled back like a wave, but just for an instance the drops of milk still gleamed, their fall sending tiny ripples of light across the pitch-black sky…

"Beautiful…" Aunt Bea whispered. Then the circle closed up and the stars were gone. No light, no milk, no nothing: like a door closing in a great black barn. The fog returned and all of a sudden the world seemed to put on weight, the ship made of wood, metal, *stuff*. And in that instance I suddenly realised how heavy everything was, how cumbersome – tons and tons of metal bobbing on an unlit sea.

My aunt bent down to look at me.

"Oh Alex … that was really great – I wouldn't have missed it for the world. Alex? Alex?"

I didn't say anything. Bea shivered and wrapped her long white arms around me.

"Alex? It's freezing out here. We've got to go…"

I didn't move. You could just about make out the music from the dance downstairs. The fog covered the ship as if it wanted to listen to it too.

"Alex? Come on now. It's cold…"

I was watching a woman in a long black dress standing staring out to sea. How still she seemed! Like she was made of wood or nailed to the prow of the boat. Looking at her it was impossible to imagine her ever moving again.

"Alex?"

The woman must have been frozen solid: I couldn't see her face or her expression but her dress seemed very stiff.

"Alex?"

Aunt Bea was right; it was very cold. She put her hand on my shoulder and led me back down through the hatch. As soon as we were back inside the fog covered everything – the deck, the woman, the ship. And that was that.

4

After "the night of a million stars", two different rumours started to gain currency: the first that we were nearly there, the second that there were considerably fewer passengers on board than when we'd first set off. The proof was "right before your eyes" (Mrs Normand). You didn't need to wait nearly so long for your tray, there were a lot more potatoes left, and as for the tennis courts – why, they were pretty much deserted! But where would everybody go? The sea was a great grey car park, the fog as solid as cement. Mr Williams, the chiropodist, was having none of it: everything was so dull, he said, it was just that more people were staying in their cabins these days. Fog, fog and more fog: what was there to see anyway? One day was like a charcoal drawing of the next. Meals, drinks, dances: they came and they went and all the time the fog covered us like a shroud…

And what of the other rumour: that we were nearly there, almost "the other side of the pond" (Uncle Glyn)? Sightings of that "further shore" were common but never seemed to amount to anything: it was like somebody had sketched out the sea but forgotten to draw in the coast. Mrs Davis said that if the water was getting choppier it meant that we were near to land, but Mr Sklandowsky argued just the opposite: the bigger the waves the deeper the sea. "Does the sea have a deep and a shallow end?" I asked, but Mikey said no, it was more like a bathtub, though without the taps. "No bath ever made me feel this sick," complained my father, the mariner. Dad's face was the colour of gruel. His clothes didn't seem to fit him. He walked like he was a hundred and two. According to Uncle Glyn, he looked like he was "fixing to get his shoes shined in a funeral parlour".

I didn't know though, maybe Mr Sklandowsky was right: maybe it *was* just the seasickness that was keeping everyone indoors. According to Michael it was a hundred yards between toilets on the outer decks, and for many this was a shit too far. Besides there were rumours of some kind of sick-bug sweeping through the passenger quarters: was this why C and D Decks had been closed down too? Dad couldn't even get to his lookout post, but at least that meant that the gulls left him alone. "About time too," complained Mum. "They've ruined that coat!" Instead Dad would shuffle up to the barrier and watch the cleaning crews and their mops, teams of stewards rigorously swabbing every inch of the "prohibited" levels. But what had happened to all the people whose cabins were on C or D? Could they all be ill? "Little lamb, there's nothing to worry about," said Mrs Andrews, reassuringly. "Just don't eat the fish."

I couldn't tell if Mum was sick or not. Sometimes she fussed over Dad, loading him up with blankets and cushions, but other times she flew off the handle, berating him for "spoiling her one and only trip". Most of the time though, she sat in a big chair with her book.

"What's it about?" I asked.

"Russia," she said. "There's lots of snow. Tanya is unhappy. Tyurin still hasn't come."

In the main lounge Uncle Glyn did magic tricks for all the little kids, whilst Auntie Bea handed out sweets. I helped out from time to time, and Uncle Glyn would magically produce a banana from my ear, or pretend my tongue was a piece of ham and pull it out with a pair of pliers. Such fun! Kids flocked to Uncle Glyn like pigeons to a sandwich. When he played 'What's The Time Mr Wolf?' you could hear the screaming all the way from the poop deck.

I met Bethan there and afterwards we went off to knock over the stewards' buckets. I could tell that her heart wasn't in it though. We didn't even mess up the bit they'd cleaned; instead Bethan just sat down and looked at her knees. How mournful she looked! Like some kind of orphan in a mawkish little book. When I asked her what was wrong she jumped to her feet and chased me along A Deck with a knitting needle. O Bethan! When I got back to my cabin I had a nosebleed, but it stopped after a while. The view from my porthole was still grey. The ship went up and down like the sea was full of stairs.

When I went back out I found Mikey playing chess with Dr Kutchner, the two of them staring at the board like it was the last square of dry land in the world. The few strands of hair stuck to Dr Kutchner's head made it look like a cracked egg.

"Move now please," he said, staring intently at Mikey's horse.

Michael looked uncertain. "But if it's food poisoning, how come only certain decks have come down with it? Or is it something on just these decks?"

Dr Kutchner shrugged.

"Seasickness?" asked Mikey, moving a prawn.

"Ah, you are dreaming I think. And the people? Where are the people?"

"Well, confined to their cabins, of course. Where else would they be?"

Dr Kutchner narrowed his eyes.

"Ah! Perhaps you are not such a clever boy, I think. Check!"

Mikey furrowed his brow and moved another piece.

"You think they all fell overboard?" he asked.

"When you say another word, I am angry," hissed Dr Kutchner, looking down at the board.

Mabel and her mother were seated in sun-loungers just across the way, Mabel staring forlornly at Michael, Mrs Mook still writing postcards. What on earth did she find to write about? A whole stack of pictures of the White Star liner were propped up in her blanket, her fingers stained blue with the ink. That was nothing compared to her daughter, mind; Mabel looked like she'd been rubbing coal around her eyes and her lips were painted on like a clown's. She still looked sort-of pretty though. Not that my brother so much as looked in her direction. Poor Mabel! Her whole body drooped like a plant in need of water.

"So," said Michael, his accent unconsciously mimicking Dr Kutchner. "Do you think we're actually going anywhere? I mean, the ship is moving, but I've done my calculations, and the bay can't be that wide…"

"Imbecile! Now, move your piece please."

Mikey examined the board.

"But how far can it be? We can't be going in a straight line. And without the sun it's impossible to know…"

"That is not so important, I think. No, the real question is: is there another side?"

Mikey looked at him strangely.

"If our side, why not theirs?"

"Theirs?"

"Well, the White Star staff for a start…"

Dr Kutchner looked at a passing steward contemptuously.

"They are not so different from you or I, I think. In the morning they think 'where is my breakfast' and at night 'where is my dinner?'."

"You don't think they've even been there?"

"There? Where is 'there'? Move piece now, stupid boy."

By the sun-loungers, Mr and Mrs Thomas came and sat down next to Mrs Mook. The two of them had been standing over at the railings, staring hand in hand at the mist. Mrs Thomas looked rather flushed.

"Yes, the fog is definitely a different shade over there," she said. "We must be almost there…"

Mrs Mook nodded. "Oh I hope so, my dear. I need to get these off…" and she gestured absent-mindedly at the postcards scattered all around her.

"I pack up my things every morning," whispered Mrs Thomas, as if divulging some deep, dark secret. "Just in case…"

"It pays to be ready!" said Mrs Mook. "Mabel, move over, give the lady and gentleman some room. And stop staring into space, dear, people will think you're simple…"

Mabel moodily pulled her long legs in and arranged her painted mouth into a miserable little pout. She still looked pretty though.

"Imbecile!" shouted Dr Kutchner.

That night, Michael and I had to go to dinner with Aunt Bea and Uncle Glyn 'cause Mum had a headache and Dad was feeling sick. The first course was lobster-bisque which was very orange. After dinner there was dancing and Uncle Glyn yelled, "I do declare the captain's balls get bigger every year!" Then Mikey and I went back to our cabins. I pretended to be a dog for a bit, and then I put the lights out and went to sleep.

It was a strange night, though. After I nodded off I dreamt about Grandy and Auntie Glad and in my dream they were locked up someplace dark, someplace like a hold, and the space was slowly filling with water. The water was the colour of ink and before long the whole room was filled in like a colouring book. How full it seemed! When I woke up my pyjamas were wet and my bed smelt a little too. It was also very cold. When I thought about all that black water sloshing around in the hold I started to shiver so I got up and dumped my pyjama bottoms in the corner of the room. It was awful late and the boat ("ship!") was going up and down like a lift. Then, just as I was skipping back to my bed, I nearly jumped out of my skin; something was knocking, knocking hard, right on my cabin door. Straight away I thought of Grandy: had he somehow managed to escape and find his way up to the higher deck? I imagined him and Auntie Glad, pulling themselves up out of the strange black ink, their legs all sodden and stained. But then I thought of Dr Beagle:

what if he'd woken up hungry and gone to look for a tasty morsel to get him through the night – a tasty morsel like me? I pulled the covers up to my chin and thought about the pictures in my fairy-tale book. Tch, what should I do? I crept out from my cold, wet bed and reluctantly shuffled toward the door. Ah me – if only I'd kept my bottoms on! But when I pulled open the door it was just Bethan in her 'little princess' pyjamas, her hair curled up in two little horns and her face as white as a sheet.

"Alex?" she said. "Alex, you've got to come. Mummy and Daddy have gone!"

"Gone?"

"You've got to come!" she yelled, pulling me out of the cabin and into the cold and draughty corridor. Who would have believed such a little girl could be so strong? It was very windy out, especially without bottoms.

There wasn't anyone around, though: at this time of night the deck was completely deserted. All the doors were closed. Only a few bulbs were still lit. Bethan's face was terribly puffy and her eyes were red from crying.

"But where should they go?" I asked Bethan, shivering in the cold night air.

"When I woke up they'd vanished," Bethan said in a strange croaky voice that wasn't like her at all. "Mummy said she wasn't feeling very well and then she lay down and then she was gone altogether."

We crossed A Deck and ran down to B Deck, our two little shapes the only things moving onboard the ship that night. What a pair! My feet were getting kind-of dirty and that made me think about the night before we sailed, the night I walked out to the sea-wall looking for Dad. The fog looked just the same.

"Here!" said Bethan. "Come see!"

The cabin-door was open but I couldn't see any sign of life. The cabin – considerably bigger and posher than my parents' room, I noted – was all in darkness, the space "dark as the devil's bum-hole" (Cousin Ted). The sheets were pulled back on the high double bed but otherwise the room looked completely normal. I didn't know what to do: Bethan was crying quite a bit by now, and needed to blow her nose badly.

"Maybe they're still out dancing…"

Bethan kept on sobbing.

"Or maybe they've gone to look for something to eat…"

She looked at me despairingly. "Alex?"

"Let's go get my mum and dad, Bethan. They'll know what to do. My dad's an electrician…"

We left the cabin and tried retracing out steps. Yellow tape blocked the stairs down to C Deck and I thought about Grandy and Auntie Glad again, and my dream of the rising tide. The way back to A Deck felt endless. It was very quiet.

"It's alright Bethan," I said. "My dad has walked every inch of this ship. He'll know where to look…"

Bethan was sniffling hard, but at least she was still following me. Her hair was stuck to her face like spaghetti.

"My father, the rationalist!" I said proudly, but Bethan wasn't listening. Still, at least she wasn't crying; instead she wiped her nose angrily on her sleeve.

When we finally got to Mum and Dad's door I stopped and banged on the door as hard as I could. I paused, tried again, but no – nothing. We tried pushing at it but it was locked. Not knowing what to do we knocked again and then started kicking the door with our bare feet. Not a sausage! Bethan looked at me with big frightened eyes and I said that my mummy and daddy were very heavy sleepers but that we should go and find my big brother Michael, who was very good at sums. Bethan nodded from under her hair. Her eyes were two round balls.

For some reason Michael's door was wide open. Michael wasn't there though. His covers were pulled back and despite Michael being the neatest boy in the whole world, his clothes were strewn across his bed with a nest of coat hangers lying willy-nilly on the floor. My stomach gave a long, high-pitched yip. "Maybe he's gone dancing too…" I said.

Bethan nodded.

"Maybe everybody's gone dancing…"

Truth be told though, I was worried. I mean, what if Bethan and I were the only two souls left onboard? No stewards, no cleaners, no passengers; not even the captain and Able Seaman Able. But where had they all gone? Could they all have dropped off the side?

We wandered up and down the corridors but all seemed equally deserted. Ditto the lounge and the 'adults-only' bar. There weren't any grown-ups anywhere. The boat was as empty as a sieve.

"Bethan? Bethan, shall we have a look up on deck? It's alright Bethan, don't cry, everybody's waiting for us somewhere…"

We bumbled around the corridors for what seemed like ages before finding a set of stairs and a hatch opening outwards. As soon as we started to get near to the deck I felt my pyjama top wanting to float off, and watched helplessly as Bethan's hair started to rise up in two little horns. Ah that power, that force, that pull toward … what? And then I heard myself say, "Look, Bethan, stars…" and I knew it had all happened again, just like before...

Yes, the sky was clear now, just thin wisps of fog like fine white hairs, floating listlessly above the boat. Behind them I could see my old friends the stars, little beacons showing the way across. Ah, how happy I felt – the stars were still there, and the rest of the sky too!

"Bethan," I said. "Bethan, its okay…"

"What's that?" she said. "Alex, what's that?"

She wasn't looking at the stars but instead seemed to be listening to a series of loud bangs and thuds coming from around the next corner, each sudden clunk making her jump and start.

"Alex?"

Ah me, were those footsteps? Or were they something else entirely?

"It must be your mum and dad. Let's see Bethan, let's go see…"

We followed the bangs and the clatters and turned the corner in time to see a bunch of oddly dressed figures rushing to look at something on the other side, men in dressing gowns, women in overcoats, some folk still in their nightwear. As soon as I saw them a great wave of relief washed over me: we weren't the only ones left, there were still others on board after all!

"Look Bethan," I said. "Look over there…"

It was only when we rounded the corner and saw the great huddle of topcoats, scarves and fleeces that we realised just what it was that everybody was staring at: the further shore, the other side at last…

It's true! The fog had faded away to almost nothingness, and ahead of us you could make out a luminous white wall, like the edge of a page. Parts of the wall looked as smooth as if they'd been built by hand, whilst other sections were crumbling away into a fine, silvery powder, trickling down the cliffs in little grey streams. What a view, what a sight! From where we were standing the shore looked like an enormous eye-lid, with deep black shadows for lashes, a massive expanse of white, and cracked grey wrinkles at each corner. But what if the eye should open? Shafts of calm, white light poured down between the gorges, whilst at the bottom piles of silvery dust gathered in the craters like snow. Behind the cliffs we could glimpse other vast formations, some grey, some white, some almost yellow in the strange frosted light. It was like peering at the world through a huge chunk of ice, though everything was dry, powdery, like a kid's chalk drawing. Ah me, was the other side made of dust and ash? And that's when I saw Michael.

He was standing with everybody else, a cagoule on over his PJs and a hat Granny Dwyn had knitted jammed firmly on his head. When he saw me he looked me up and down and sighed.

"Alex," he said, "Alex, where are your pants?"

I didn't know what to say. Everybody was pointing at the other side and talking in high, excited voices. You could make out more details now, little dark clusters that might have been houses or hills or maybe just holes. A fine, dry snow started falling over us. The colour of the cliffs kept changing. I could still feel the pull of the great darkness above me, but I held onto the rails and refused to look up. When I turned round, I could see Bethan's little body making its way through the crush, searching for her mum and dad amongst all the dressing gowns and raincoats and waterproofs. She dodged between two stewards with fuzzy lips, and then I watched her zigzag between an enormous woman in her nightie and two old dears in identical brown coats. How tiny she looked, with her mop of blonde hair and her little red bod! Then she disappeared into the crowd and I never saw her again.

Schröter's Valley

1

The main thing I remember about the hotel was that it was very, very pale. Rather than one tall building, as I'd always imagined, it was made up of a cluster of little short ones, funny-looking pre-fabs scattered around a squat central block. Uncle Glyn said it was "pretty as an abattoir" but the bluish-grey snow softened it a little, and there were some cosy-looking lamps lit in some of the windows. When we arrived it was still night and the air was very cold. A hand-painted sign ('HOTEL LA LUNA') had been nailed to the front of the main block, though the last two letters only just managed to fit on.

Trudging doggedly through the snow, nobody looked very happy. Where were the "facilities, the activities, the sights of special scientific interest?" (Dad). Aunt Bea took off her sun glasses. "If this is first prize, I wouldn't like to see second!" Before getting off the bus we'd been given strange heavy shoes that made it look like we were going bowling; neither Aunt Bea nor Mum were keen on wearing them but what could you do? It was "mandatory" (Michael), as was having some kind of liquid smeared on your tongue, a kind of minty milk (I went round twice).

When we got inside, the lobby looked suspiciously like a doctor's waiting room; rows of plastic garden chairs had been set up, and some fella with a handle-bar moustache half-heartedly handed us a ticket as we tramped past. It was a bit depressing, to be honest, the plants dead, the floor unwashed and the heater giving off a very strange smell.

"What now?" asked Aunt Bea.

"It's a waiting room, so wait" (Uncle Glyn).

The chairs weren't very comfortable though. Awkward backs, broken hinges: and the height, so low!

"Isn't there anybody working here?" asked Mr Begham from the hardware shop. "Didn't anyone tell them we were coming?"

The fella behind the desk didn't seem to care. "That swine," whispered Uncle Glyn. "He wouldn't piss on you if your feet were on fire!" Instead, the fella just scratched his 'tache and laid his head in his hands, scribbling half-heartedly on the pad in front of him. Poor us! Mum took out her book and Michael started on some homework while I made funny popping noises with my cheeks. When would we be allowed to go? "When the mouse buries the cat!" (Granny Dwyn). Even Uncle Glyn fell quiet. "Wee wee, widdley-wee," I said and Mikey said, "Shhh!"

Minutes crept by, tens of minutes, years. Then, just when it seemed that nothing would ever happen again, the manager suddenly appeared, accompanied by his beard, two ladies and a trolley. The fella looked awful familiar and I immediately thought of Dr Boney; he was likewise tall, imposing, and stroked his beard as if it were a large dog. How scary he looked! Then he strode to the front of the queue and spoke to us in a loud, booming voice.

"Ladies and gentlemen," he said. "Boys and girls…"

It's funny though – despite the great impression he made on me I can't remember a single word of what he said: something about wearing the right footwear, I think, and staying within designated areas. Uncle Glyn wasn't impressed. "He's so full of it his boots squeak," he hissed, all the time helping himself to biscuits from the trolley. The rest of us collected our tea from the urn and hovered uncertainly to one side. There was only one porter, an old stooped fella with a stubbly beard and a bent back, and he moved very, very slowly – "like a snail with corns" (Mum). Dad picked up our suitcases but where should we go – back to the boat? We milled around with everybody else until Michael finally worked out that the numbers on the tickets referred to the dormitories up the stairs, draughty halls divvied up into 'rooms' by a series of curtains on rails. It wasn't "exactly a palace" (Mum), but everyone felt too tired to kick up a fuss. We placed our stuff in the little lockers and went looking for our allotted space; my tummy was "empty as a bum's lunch pail" (Grandy), my legs just about ready to drop. My bed – some kind of makeshift cot – squeaked terribly, but it could have been worse: Mikey struggled to even fit on his bed, while Mum and Dad had to push two of them together. "For this, two stars?" (Mum). The pillow was thin and the blanket "not entirely warm" (Mr Wallace). Still, what did we expect, the Ritz? We scrunched up our eyes and thought, 'What can you do, what did we think, tch, maybe it will all look different in the morning…'

But when we woke up, the stars were still out and the sky still looked terribly black. It was hard to say how long we'd been under: we all felt stiff from the cot-beds and most folk hadn't even bothered to undress. Still, "man has to eat" (Granny May), so we all mooched off to the 'great hall' (in reality a dismal cafeteria) for our vast "repast". Surprisingly though, the food was really nice. I polished one bowl of porridge and then went back for another. It's true what they say

– 'Feed the belly and legs come with it!' Outside, fat flakes of cobalt-blue snow drifted past the windows, their roundy blobs completely different from the silvery dust earlier. Rather than charcoal these looked like big blobs of paint.

Dad had big bags under his eyes. Mum was still wearing the same make-up. Aunt Bea's hair stuck up like a bird with a broken wing. Only Mikey, Uncle Glyn and I scoffed down our food with great gusto.

"This stuff is terrible," said Uncle Glyn. "But such big portions!"

Mum gazed out at the snow as if in a trance. She didn't even say anything when I licked my bowl and got porridge all over my nose.

"The most important thing is to get us moved," said Dad, stroking his unshaven chin. "We can't stay in this place for long…" Uncle Glyn agreed. "No wallflower ever walked out of the garden!"

Unfortunately when we trooped back to the reception hall, the queue at the information desk snaked right around the lobby. No matter what the question, the fella always had the same answer: there had been some problems getting the hotel ready in time but guests had to bear with them. "I'd bare more than that if the curtain fell down!" (Aunt Bea). What a *schwein*, what a creep! But there was no getting round him. The manager was "indisposed". No other rooms were available. Was it his fault if some of the cots were broken?

Whilst Dad tried to sort things out, Mikey and I went out into the garden (not that there were any plants or grass or anything) to "kick our heels". I wanted to play snowballs but my aim wasn't so good and Michael seemed more interested in the chemical composition of the snow. "Hmm," he said, scrunching it up in his fingers, "curious…" My brother, the scientist! He rolled it this way and that, seeing which bits crumbled and which bits stuck. "It tastes funny too," I said, rolling on my back.

Afterwards we walked down the little hill to the high wall that marked the boundary of the complex and the strange white world beyond. How big the sky seemed! There were so many stars up there, they'd forgotten to leave space for the moon.

"Michael," I said. "Why is it still night, even though we've been to bed?"

His eyes scanned the horizon as if he'd been copying Seaman Able.

"Well, what time is it?"

I looked at my watch.

"Do I start with the big hand or the little one?"

"The little one."

"It's not moving."

"Mm. Must be something to do with the magnetic pull."

"Pully?"

"Pull."

"But how will we know when it's dinner-time?"

"I'm sure that belly of yours will know…"

Mikey walked down to the main gate in his bowling-shoes and watched the funny snow falling over the valley. He suddenly looked very small, silhouetted against all that nothing. "This way to the dandruff mine!" (Uncle Glyn).

"Mikey? Will it ever get light?"

"That depends how far North we've come."

"North?"

"Oh, and the time of year, of course…"

"But haven't we just come across the bay? Mikey? Mikey?"

Mikey didn't say anything. The stars turned and wheeled. The snow looked almost violet in the strange unearthly light.

After lunch the bus returned to take guests back down to the beach. Dad didn't feel very well though, and besides, he wanted to go and look for the manager and his beard. Mikey stayed and did some sums and I played 'worms' and 'shark-food' on the terrace. Still, it didn't sound like we'd missed much. Mrs Mook said the sea had been "black as the devil's bath water" and that there was nothing else to see but the fog. Worse, Mabel had fallen and grazed her knee. Mabel looked at Michael beseechingly but he was busy with his equations and wouldn't even inspect her scab.

After dinner, there was a dance, just like the ones onboard ship. In fact, in many ways it felt as if we were all back there: Aunt Bea danced with one of the waiters, Uncle Glyn spilled wine down his front, Dad mooched about on his own. I looked out of the window, half expecting to see huge black waves, but no: all that was out there was snow. There was something about the 'great hall' (the canteen) that made me think it was just like the ship's ballroom – or maybe it was just that the band was the same, who knows? Anyway most people were pretty tired from lack of sleep and the dancing petered out fairly early. All of us – Aunt Bea, the Thomases, Mr Chattarji, the optimist ("optician!") – we all went to bed wondering if the sun would remember to rise in the morning. It was a very long night; my cot-bed creaked and Dad's breathing sounded awful. When we woke up it was still dark. We stared up at the sky but couldn't even recognise it. The stars seemed to go on forever.

"Am I getting up or going to bed?" I asked.

"You're getting up," said Dad. "Put your socks on…"

"But how come it's the same day?"

"It's not the same day," he said sleepily.

"Is it tomorrow?"

"Yes Alex."

"Today tomorrow or tomorrow tomorrow?"

"Alex, where are your socks?"

At breakfast it was announced that the kids' club (somebody had drawn a poster, but really badly) was to meet in the 'recreation room' for 'games and supervised activity'. I didn't want to go but Mum was adamant: I needed to 'mix with other children' and 'have some fun'. When I got there, the 'recreation room' turned out to be a store cupboard full of cleaning stuff. There was only one other kid, a scrawny looking boy with almost no hair, and we stared at each other for a bit and then sat down and hugged our knees. We stayed like that for a long time.

It turned out that the kid's name was Hwyl, and he was here with his mum. The two of them had been sick nearly all the way coming but he was 'a bit better now'. He didn't look well though – half a bag of nothing and light as a paper bag. Still, he knew how to open childproof tops so we opened up all the cleaning fluids and started to mix up some of the chemicals.

"Do you want a magic potion?" I asked.

"Yes please!"

"Do you want to fly?"

"Yes please!"

"Open wide!"

I was just about to pour it in when the door opened and a strict-looking woman in a lab-coat came marching in.

"Kidzone?" she said, in a bored tone of voice.

"No sir, kids' club," I said, putting down the bottle of bleach.

She looked down at a clipboard and scowled. "This way."

We were led down a side-corridor to a little white room with a bed and a bright, glary light.

"Right, who's first?" she said. "Alex?"

"He's Alex," I said and Hwyl was picked up and plonked on the bed, his little legs swinging from the side.

"Right now Alex, roll up your sleeve."

"Is this a game?"

"We need to see how you're feeling now…"

"Mummy says I'm excused games."

"Just a few tests…"

"I've got a note…"

"Roll up your sleeve Alex."

Ah me – who would have guessed that Hwyl would be so full of blood? He was crying quite loudly but Mrs Bushy-Brows didn't seem fazed. She shone a light in his eyes, pulled down his eyelids, and then smeared some more of that stuff on his tongue.

"Urgh," he said, pulling a face.

"Don't be a baby," she said. "Right. Now breathe into this." And she handed him some kind of tube, though I couldn't see where it led. He immediately started to choke.

"Breathe not suck! Idiot child."

Hwyl's cheeks were a funny colour but he did his best.

"Good … good … right, that's enough," said the woman. "Okay Alex, you can get down now. Hwyl?"

I looked around, the very picture of innocence. "I'm not Hwyl."

She stared intently at her clipboard and then back at me. My face was bright red.

"Not Hwyl…"

"No sir…"

"But then, what…"

"Sir?" I said very seriously, making my face as earnest as I possibly could. "I think there's been some kind of terrible mistake."

After the 'tests' we were given a lolly and a sticker and hustled into an empty room to play with a beanbag. "I think that goo tastes great," I whispered but Hwyl still wouldn't talk to me. I popped the beanbag under my bottom. "Look Hwyl, I've done a poo!" It was quite a long morning. When we were finally let out it was lunchtime and Hwyl went off to the canteen to find his mum. At the far table I could see Michael sitting with Auntie Bea and Uncle Glyn. Dad was still looking for the manager. No one knew where Mum was – "Vladivostok, maybe?" (Uncle Glyn).

Whilst everybody was filling his or her faces I looked down at the plaster on my arm. The woman said it was going to be used for 'tests' and I hoped I'd pass. The food was D-licious. I waved at Hwyl sitting

74

with his mum, but he didn't wave back. By the time I'd finished dessert my bowl was so clean I could see my face in it. "Hungry?" asked Aunt Bea watching me scrape desperately on the bottom.

That afternoon's 'excursion' was a walking-tour to 'Crater Billy', the big round hole next to the hotel. Uncle Glyn went off to find the free bar and Auntie Bea wanted a lie-down, but Mikey and I tagged along. It wasn't far, though you had to watch your footing on all the snowy blobs. Everyone was given a big yellow windcheater and a whistle. Mabel was there, limping a little, walking alongside her mum.

The hole ('crater!') turned out to be enormous, with really steep sides. Our guide – a pimply-faced guy with a bum-fluff moustache – warned us not to get too close and to keep our whistle to hand at all times. At the bottom there were blobs of black and blobs of bluey-grey – nothing else at all. A few of the townsfolk took photographs and Mr Whalley picked out a rock for a memento, but I couldn't really work out what the fuss was.

"Can I slide down to the bottom?"

"No."

"Can I jump down from the sides?"

"No."

"Can I throw rocks?"

In the end I wound up playing hide and seek by myself amongst the spindly trees but it wasn't much fun. Mabel kept making big eyes at Michael, but Michael only had eyes for that hole. "Just imagine the energy released in the impact!" he said. Mabel was wearing funny brown lipstick, like she'd been eating chocolate all afternoon, but she still looked very pretty. Mrs Mook watched her gazing at Michael and sighed. "Mabel, keep your head *up!*" she called.

Back at the hotel Dr Morgan had lost his clothes and was sitting in the lobby looking cross. He'd been finishing off his crossword and "not bothering anyone", when some "stern-faced bint" in a white coat had pounced on him, claiming that it was time for "hydro-therapy" in the "wet room". The next thing he knew he was squatting in a pool of brown water, smelling "like a fart in a lift". Poor Dr Morgan! He didn't even get his clothes back but instead was given a White Star bathrobe and a pair of slippers and led back into the lobby, dripping. His robe wasn't quite long enough, though we tried not to look. "An outrage!" he spluttered, trying to cover himself up. His knees were the colour of tea.

What could you do? Nobody had seen the manager since that first night. Dad had gone up the stairs to find his office but it seemed to have vanished: there was nothing in his room but a sink and a chair. "What kind of an establishment is this?" he asked. "Where are the facilities?" Dad had other worries too: he hadn't seen Mum since the morning and she hadn't even turned up at lunch. She'd been reading her book and then disappeared. Dad took Michael and I to one side. "Your mother, Alex, she's … *excitable*," he said to us, patting me gently on the head. Mrs Mook thought she had seen her "near the solarium", but that was hours ago and it might not have been Mum anyway. We all felt a bit strange but luckily Mum turned up again when it was time for dinner. No one would tell me where Mum had been or what was wrong though. She looked kind-of pale and her eyes were bright and wet.

"Mum?" I said. "Where do you go to when you're sad? Is it Russia?"

"Sad? Why sad?" she asked, stroking my hair erratically.

After dinner, Mum and Aunt Bea danced with all the waiters – even the one with the pointy beard. One of the waiters seemed very keen on Aunt Bea, but she kept shaking her head and had to pull her fingers out of his paw. Afterwards Mum wanted to go outside to look at the stars. Dad said it was too cold but Mum went anyway. What was Dad to do? He followed her even though he felt "rougher than a cow's tongue" (Granny Dwyn). They stood there in the middle of the garden, gazing up at all that dark. 'Just think,' I thought looking at them: 'all those stars up in heaven and only one Mummy and one Daddy!' Mum had bluey snow in her hair. Something purple was dripping from Dad's nose. Then they came back in and it was time for bed.

I couldn't sleep much though. There were too many noises and people moving around and what sounded like a bell tolling someplace far away. Once again I felt I was back on the boat, my cot rolling gently with the waves. I closed my eyes and it was as if I were bobbing up and down, softly swaying 'pon the "endless, briny hills" (Uncle Tomos). But where was our little seaside town? It seemed very far behind us now: the school, the church and the shopping precinct – all had fallen overboard, swept away by the big black waves. What a thought! No more shops, no more houses, no Knob Rock – just this black and bottomless ocean. I pulled my blanket all the way up to my chin and waited for the water. No house, no garden, no bed to sleep in; little mother, I whispered – where would we all go then?

2

The next day we went on a bus trip to the 'Lake of Sleep'. Dr Morgan couldn't come because his clothes still hadn't turned up, and the Micklewhites and the Thomases were staying behind for 'special treatment', but I was very keyed up. All the way there I kept singing, 'There was a man who had a dog/And Bingo was his name-o!' and kicking the seat in front of me. The bus was very hot. Everyone had to put on a big yellow jacket and the bus stank "like a plastic nappy" (Uncle Glyn). Little mother, what a sweat! The windows were steamed up by the time we left the hotel, and no one could see a thing (though of course it was still dark anyway...).

The lake turned out to be a big tear-shaped stretch of water circled by more of those skinny white trees. The lake itself was pretty much frozen, the ice very, very black. Most of the snow was a silvery colour, though the odd dab was mauve or even purple. Where was all this stuff coming from? Such colours, such tints! But then "even winter dreams of spring!" (Aunt Bea).

The adults all congregated by the finger-trees, where a picnic had been laid out on squares of plastic sheeting. Mum took photos of the pale, spindly trees, with the black lake in the background: then we had to line up for a photo too. "Quick, pretend you're happy!" yelled Mum. I wandered in and out of the trees blowing my whistle until it was taken off me and I was given a scotch egg instead. For some reason it tasted of that goo they kept giving us but I didn't mind. "What filleth the mouth feedeth the soul!" (Granny Mair).

After that Uncle Glyn pretended to be the Abominable Snowman and the kids all tried to bury him. "I think Mr Abominable needs a sit down," said Aunt Bea, and the two of them went off behind a big rock and ate sausage rolls. Dad and Michael had gone off for a trek up to a nearby crag; when they came back Mikey was talking about glacial erosion and Dad was limping. Mikey's pockets were full of "samples" he had collected from the "geological site". They made his trousers bulge and Mum was worried about the lining.

Mabel was there too, wearing her mum's long blue evening dress under her big yellow wind-cheater. Whilst Mikey and Dad were off at the rock, she sat down next to me, her head seeming too heavy for her neck.

"You're Michael's brother, aren't you?"

"I call him Mikey," I said, burying my feet in the snow.

"Does he like that?" she asked, an intense look on her face.

"No," I said, watching the snow cover my trouser slops. Mabel's hair was half way between a bonfire and a bird's nest, with all sorts of spikes and plastic ornaments perched in it.

"He seems very smart," she said, not looking at me but at the skinny trees instead.

"He can do long-division and everything," I replied, trying to think of another kind of maths. "Fractions too."

Mabel nodded.

"My brother, the mathematician!"

"Will you give him this?" she said and with that she unzipped her puffer jacket and retrieved a slim white envelope.

"When I draw numbers, I give them little faces. Do you do that too?"

"Don't give it to him here though," she said. "Only give it to him when we get back to the hotel. You won't forget now will you? Give it to Michael when we get back to the hotel."

"Number four has got a long nose…"

79

"You're a bright boy, right?"

"That's a nice dress," I said. "Is it your mum's?"

"You won't forget the letter?"

"My mum has a black dress and a blue one…"

"Um…"

"I'd like to wear my mum's dresses too…"

"I better go now. Don't lose the letter, okay? There's a big boy…"

And with that she pulled her dress down below her puffer jacket and slipped away. Ah, what an angel, what a doll! I thought about opening the envelope there and then, but I figured it might have big words in it, so I decided to let Mikey read it to me sometime later instead.

It was very exciting talking to Mabel and afterwards I had to get up and go for a walk. Dad was resting by the bus. Aunt Bea and Uncle Glyn were playing 'shark' with the little kids (Uncle Glyn was 'it'). Mum was alone, staring at the trees. The trees were like white pencils, sharpened at the top. No one saw me go and I sang to myself 'Alex, Alex/where did you go?/Behind the trees/to meet your beau…'

Past the clearing, the path cut between two banks of purplish snow and then forked in two: one path led up to the rocks (boring!), the other back down to the lakeside, past black reed-beds and clumps of sharp, thistly grass. You had to be careful this way though 'cause the ground was very soft and the only way you could get through was by jumping from tuft to tuft. I wondered whether I'd see any birds or animals but I didn't. What kind of animals would live on the other side anyway? Polar bears, penguins, wolves… The stars gleamed brightly, and it wasn't that dark when you got used to it – more like dusk. Maybe that was why the snow seemed violet and blue. There was no sign of the sun anywhere. 'Like wearing a black hat!' I thought.

At the edge of the lake the ice melted into dark, brackish water, with all sorts of twigs and funny blobs floating in it. I followed the edge for a while, though to be honest, my bowling shoes were pretty wet by now 'cause I kept slipping in the clay. The murk made a funny popping noise when I pulled my foot out.

"Plop, plop, plop!" I chanted.

Looking back I could still see the bus and the trees and all the yellow figures in their puffer jackets standing to one side. It didn't look all that far – about twice as long as my arm. But across on the other side of the lake it was harder to see. It was darker there, and the shapes might have been anything: trees, rocks or thick black daubs. I watched the blobs moving around for a while, waiting for them to form things, but they didn't seem to want to: it was very fuzzy and very dark. After a while I thought I could make out some kind of building over there, its shape oddly familiar, like a house I'd been to many times, but I couldn't really be sure. Was it Grandy's? I opened my eyes as wide as they would go. The house was hazy and dark and badly painted but looked more and more like Grandy's the longer I stared at it. But what was it doing here? Had someone taken it to bits and carried it all over in the ship's hold? Had someone copied it? I took another step and then realised I was on the ice. It was kind of slippery. When I looked down it was like looking down at a great big hole, but I wasn't worried. The closer I got to the other side, the clearer Grandy's house became. Yes, there was his wall, his shed, his garage with its roof caving him. 'Grandy/grandy/old and stooped/ his beard is long/and his body pooped'.

"Grandy!" I yelled. "Grandy are you there?"

I was quite a way out now. You might think that the stars would be reflected in the black ice, but they weren't. Beneath my feet there was just a big empty hole. I edged out further and could hear my heart thumping away. Such a long way down!

"Hold on Grandy, I'm coming," I said, my special shoes slipping and sliding. It was very hard to keep your balance out there; one foot went one way and one foot went the other. How were you supposed to make your way across? It was as "slippery as slug polish" (Cousin Dai) and terribly cold to boot.

"Grandy, Grandy, it's Alex!" I screamed.

Then all of a sudden one foot seemed to drop and I felt my knee hit the ice. What had happened? There was a loud cracking noise and all around me everything seemed to shift. For a moment I felt very confused, but then I righted myself. My feet felt a little wet. When I looked up his house had gone and I was staring into this great bank of emptiness.

"Grandy?"

The ice shifted slightly but I managed to keep my balance. One shoe was very cold and I couldn't feel the other. I couldn't hear any more cracking but didn't dare look down. Where had Grandy's house gone to anyway – the moon?

"Grandy? Grandy where are you?"

All of a sudden I felt terribly alone. There was nothing above me and even less below. The ice seemed to move uncertainly.

"Dad!" I yelled. "Dad, Dad, Dad, Dad, Dad!"

Back by the bus one of the yellow dabs seemed to notice me and I could see several of the jackets waving. There was much gesturing and gesticulating but the bus looked an awful long way back.

"Dad!" I yelled, and with that there was an enormous bang on the ice just by me. "Daddy, come and get me…"

I looked down at the ice but couldn't see anything. Then I looked up at the sky and there wasn't anything there either. Ah, me, I thought: where does everything disappear to?

"Dadadadadadad…"

And then, as if in a fairy-story, I saw my father coming toward me, slowly picking his way across the dark ice. He was moving very gingerly and every once in a while he seemed to slip too. It took an awful long time for his voice to reach me.

"Alex, stay there," he shouted. "Don't move – I'm coming to get you."

His body slowly seemed to knit together in the gloom: his familiar gait, lurching steps, slight limp. He kept missing his footing though and I could tell that he was having trouble keeping upright on the ice.

"Alex, keep still. Stay where you are son, I'm nearly there…"

I could see his face now, his eyes and mouth and everything. Purple snow had collected on his brow and side-burns.

"Dad, I thought I could see Grandy's house but now it's gone."

"Stay right there, do you hear? Don't move a muscle."

"Dad, my shoes are very wet…"

He was no more than a few feet from me now, carefully measuring every pace and step.

"What did you think you were doing?" he growled. "Where did you think you were going?" and all of a sudden I was back on the sea-wall, staring out across the bay.

"Dad? Dad, I think I'm starting to sink…"

"Don't you do anything stupid, boy. You just stay still. Alex? Do you hear me?"

"I hear you Dad…"

I couldn't feel my feet anymore. Everything felt very unsteady.

"Alex, wait there. I'm coming to get you…"

And with that the ice around Dad loudly gave way, and with a terrible crack he disappeared into the black lake.

"Dad, Dad!" I yelled.

One second Dad's whole body was there, the next it was only his top. The sound of the ice breaking was tremendously loud.

"Dad!" I screamed.

Not knowing what to do, I closed my eyes and threw myself in after him. It was so cold I could hardly breathe. It was as if needles were being stabbed in my brain. There was a great deal of thrashing about and I could hear the sound of more and more ice breaking up.

"Alex!"

For a terrible moment I thought I could feel ice above me, like a great black road.

Either it was very dark or I was starting to pass out. But then other yellow figures appeared by our side and struggled to haul us out. One was Michael: I don't know who anybody else was. The air felt almost as cold as the drink. When we got back to the shore, Mum came rushing over and Aunt Bea and Uncle Glyn. I felt terribly worried that I'd got my special shoes all wet. Dad was coughing and shaking and struggling to stand. In my confused state I couldn't work out which was the lake and which was the sky. Everything felt cold.

"My shoes!" I cried. "My beautiful shoes!"

They felt very heavy and very wet.

All I remember about the ride back is that I got a double seat to myself and somebody gave me soup. The soup was green and I got it all down me. The next thing I knew, I was back in my bed, curled up next to flopsy dog and pushing my face into the pillow. I couldn't hear anyone else through the curtain, but whether this was because I was on my own or 'cause I had lake-water in my ears, I don't know.

The next morning (except, of course, it wasn't morning) I felt terribly achy and stiff. Mum was in her bed, but not Dad. I went over and woke Michael and he told me that Dad wasn't very well and had been taken to a different ward. I nodded solemnly, though to be honest I was still thinking about Grandy's house. Had it really been there, sitting just across the lake? But if so, how had it got there? And if Grandy's house was there, was our own house on this side also?

It was still pretty quiet in the dorm and I started to think about all my toys and comics back home and where they might be right now. I mean, if somebody had really carried our house over here then anything might have happened to them – anything! Ah me, my sticker-albums, my colouring-in books, my metal cars, all my beautiful things! What if the removals people had dropped them? What if they had all got lost? My clothes from last night were lying in a heap underneath my cot and I reached down and pulled out Mabel's letter. Unfortunately it was all scrunched up and I couldn't read anything so I threw it in the bin (I missed twice, but got it in on the third attempt). It was pretty boring just being there on my own. The snow collected outside the window like porridge. It looked awfully heavy. Every third flake was green.

I wasn't allowed to see Dad for two whole days (days?). When I did get to go to his 'special room', he looked terrible, his skin as funny looking as the snow. His thin hair was plastered to his skull and his eyes seemed very deep. 'Are you my daddy?' I thought.

"Dad," I said. "What do you think that goo is that they give us everyday? Michael says it's horrible but I think it tastes lovely…"

Dad didn't say anything: his lips looked very dry.

"Do you think it's okay if I go round twice? I mean, you don't get to go anymore so there's more to go round…"

Silence.

"Would you like me to bring you any back? I can always put some in my pocket…"

Dad shook his head and put his hand on mine. It was very cold.

"Dad?"

I didn't know what to say. His hand looked like one of Mum's old gloves.

"I'm sorry about my shoes…" I said, looking down at my feet. "Do you think I could have a new pair?"

Dad stroked my hand and made a funny kind of noise.

"Do you think they do different colours? I like red. Dad? Dad?"

He looked kind-of tired so I went out to play for a bit. Some kids were sliding down a slope on ripped bin-bags but I didn't recognise any of them and so I went off and played tag on my own instead.

When I came back in Hwyl was waiting for me in the dining hall.

"Is it true that you and your Dad fell in the ice and now he's been moved to a special ward?" he asked.

"No," I said.

His big eyes blinked, and he moved his mouth stupidly, like a fish.

"Well, that's just what I've heard."

"No."

Hwyl scratched behind his ear.

"They say that you might have to go back because you've been so naughty…"

"No."

"And all your family will have to go back too…"

I glared at him maliciously.

"Well, I heard that you had to go back to kids' club to see that woman in the white coat again…"

Hwyl's eyes practically popped out of his head.

"You haven't!"

"And that she wants to take some more blood from you 'cause your blood failed and my blood passed…"

"That's not true!"

"In fact you have to go right away…"

"You're lying," he yelled. "No one said that at all…" And with that he ran away, crying.

"Ha Ha," I said. "Ha Ha Ha." I wasn't laughing though; I was saying 'Ha Ha Ha'.

That evening, Uncle Glyn and Aunt Bea took Michael and me to the film show while Mum stayed with Dad. The film was about the biggest dog in the world, and it was very, very good. Afterwards it was fish pie for dinner, but nobody seemed to feel very hungry, and we went to look at Dad instead. He was breathing heavily and seemed fast asleep. I couldn't help noticing that his pyjamas were exactly the same colour and pattern as his sheets: grey with yellow stripes. Who knew why? I asked if I could draw on the graph paper at the bottom of his bed but Michael wouldn't let me.

"Why is Dad's tongue that colour?"

"What colour?"

"That funny grey."

"Well…"

"Is it because of the porridge?"

"Porridge?"

"The porridge they give us every day…"

"That's not porridge, it's…"

"Grey as Grandy's whiskers!"

"I…"

"Grey as a pigeon's bum!"

"Right Alex, time to go…"

The next few days were much the same. There were a few more excursions but they were all to craters so I decided not to go. Instead we all took turns watching Dad. My poor Daddy! On 'bright' days he would take some of the funny goo they kept trying to spoon into us; on 'tired' days he would sleep for hours, his chest rising and falling like the tide. 'Are you in there?' I whispered, staring up his nose.

Mum alternated between bouts of frenzied activity – packing and unpacking the suitcase, ironing all our clothes, washing her hands – and a strange kind of listlessness. Some days she looked worse than Dad: more like Bea's mum than her sister. She stopped wearing make-up or coming to 'the great hall'; she even stopped reading her Russian book. Not that this was necessarily a bad thing, of course. "Who needs more tragedy?" (Aunt Bea). Still, as the days crept by, a definite shadow fell across our holiday. Bea went to fewer and fewer dances, Uncle Glyn did less and less tricks. Michael seemed to spend more and more time scribbling figures in his notebook. "Mikey, do you want to play 'shout'?" I'd say and Aunt Bea would hiss, "Shh, he's *calculating...*"

At dinner, most of the talk revolved around the latest rumour doing the rounds: that this place wasn't the 'real' hotel, but a kind of half way house, with the proper hotel some place down the coast. Could this be true? Just think: no more sleeping in noisy dormitories! No more pills and injections! No more craters! According to Mr Vaughn, this place was just some "administrative blunder": no wonder the facilities were so poor, the blankets so thin! But in just a few days we'd all be moved out, bussed from the hotel to the genuine White Star resort. We just hoped the snow would lay off to let our bus get through...

Yes, the snow was a real worry; with each passing day more and more of the strange paint dripped down from the sky, collecting in the gutters and gumming up the windows. Some of it was blue and some of it mauve and it fell in big wet blobs before drying to a kind of hard, crumbly powder. Folk spent half the day brushing and scrubbing the paths and the other half tramping blue footprints into the carpets. Not our family though. Dad lay in bed, Mum watched Dad and Michael watched Mum. I piled snow into big heaps in the lobby. "When will we get to go to the new place?" Aunt Bea asked Uncle Glyn. "When the eggs grow feathers?"

But then one afternoon between exercise classes and group therapy, the manager reappeared, along with his beard, a clipboard and biscuits. In the same booming voice, he hoped that we had been enjoying the hotel "and all it has to offer" but also announced that the White Star Company was looking for "skilled electricians, plumbers and builders" to help with "construction work" at "our sister resort" close by. Of course, he fully appreciated that all ticket-holders were staying here as "honoured guests", but he went on to reassure candidates that "all work would be generously rewarded" and that the White Star Company would offer "special vouchers to all willing parties".

My lands, what a monstrous face he had! When he smiled his teeth looked like rocks in a great hairy sea.

Dr Morgan, still smarting over the loss of his clothes, seemed sceptical: "If they haven't finished building it yet, when do you expect to move in?" Uncle Glyn was more philosophical: "When you're working in the shit mine, why dig deeper?" I didn't know what to think: I'd just had an accident in my last clean pair of trousers. At tea, we all talked about what the new hotel might be like. "In a warmer country, let's hope!" (Aunt Bea). Would there be a swimming pool, roller-skating, an adventure playground? Everyone agreed there would.

After tea, I went off to find Hwyl. We'd patched things up and played 'Lost in the Snow' and 'Climb the Hill' practically every day. We'd both heard about the 'new' hotel and were very, very excited.

"When I get there, I'm going to go to the fairground," I said. "I've heard that the rides are all free."

"And you can go round as many times as you like!" Hwyl chimed in.

"And they last all day!"

"And you don't have to queue!"

I threw snow in the air and giggled.

"And the really big rides go as high as a mountain."

Hwyl looked impressed.

"Really?"

"As high as the sky!"

Hwyl laughed.

"As high as the moon!"

When I got back to our 'room' (which is to say, our bit of the dormitory, behind the thin beige curtain) everybody was sitting around and crying, especially Mum. Though Mum was "no stranger to tears" (Granny Mair), I'd never seen her so upset; her face was all distorted and her body shook so hard I could hear her bones rattling on the inside.

Aunt Bea and Uncle Glyn took me to one side and whispered that a pair of White Star officials had come to Dad's room and taken him away.

"Away?" I said.

"Away."

As "a skilled electrician" Dad was needed to work on the new resort, Uncle Glyn explained; he'd had to go there and then, the two fellas bundling him out of his stripy pyjamas, and swapping his bedclothes for a pair of White Star overalls and a cap.

"But why's Mum crying?" I asked, watching Mum's shoulders go up and then down.

"She doesn't think he's well enough to go," said Uncle Glyn. "But you know your father: strong as an ox and fit as a fiddle to boot…"

"He'll be fine," said Aunt Bea. "He's been looking so much better, these last few days…"

Confused, I ran straight to the lobby door, where I could see the bus for the workers waiting just outside. Other families were also there, seeing people off – plumbers, carpenters, construction workers – but I couldn't see Dad. It was really quite a scene; men with tool-boxes kissed their wives, lunchboxes were handed over, and all the little kids waved goodbye, playing games around the bus.

I looked in at each of the windows but couldn't see Dad. It was very dull in there: all the workers seemed dressed in the same kind of overalls, each carrying a toolbox and a cap. I stared and stared but it wasn't any use; as soon as the last of the workers were in their seats, the driver closed the doors and the little yellow bus slowly pulled away.

"Dad!" I shouted. "Dad?"

The bus started to turn round in front of the main building, its tyres struggling a little in the snow.

I had a better view now, but still couldn't see him.

"Dad?"

Then, just as the bus rounded the edge of the compound I suddenly spotted him, his gloomy mug mixed in amongst the joiners and the plasterers.

"Dad!" I yelled. "Dadadadadad!"

I might have been wrong though; I mean, my view was pretty poor and there were all sorts of people in the way. The bus turned a corner, the kids stopped waving and all the people went back inside. I wanted to hang around for a bit but it was kind of cold and the snow was falling in big emerald clumps. When I got back to the dorm, Michael was doing his sums, Aunt Bea and Uncle Glyn were whispering and Mum was asleep on the bed. When I looked down at her, her body was curled up like a question mark.

"Mum?" I said. "Mum?"

Her eyes flickered, but her mouth didn't so much as quiver.

"Mum, can I have Dad's porridge in the morning?" I asked, but it was no use. Her skin was pale, her eyes were red, her face as sad as Russia.

3

To "take our minds off things", Aunt Bea and Uncle Glyn took Michael and I on a ride down to the sea. It was the same bus that took us there, the same bus that took everybody everywhere. I stared at the blue and red checks and thought about all the trips it had been on, the tickets, the little ringing bell, the stops. Ah, me, I thought; who would have guessed it would end up here?

The sea was just as we'd left it: cold, wet and black. There was no sign of our boat or any kind of dock, though we might have been a bit further along the coast, who knows? We spread our blanket on the beach and looked out at the fog, its soft, grey putty gumming up the horizon. Nobody seemed to know what to do. Uncle Glyn had brought his cricket bat but didn't have a ball. The snow was all wrong for sandcastles. Even hide and seek was out – the beach seemed endlessly empty and flat.

"Who wants to go for a paddle?" asked Aunt Bea but the nurses wouldn't let us. The water didn't look very inviting anyway. "Cold as a nun's tit!" (Cousin Eugene). Instead we had races and, amazingly, I won every time. I don't know how hard everybody else was trying though.

"Aunt Bea?" I asked. "When do you think Dad will be back? I mean, will he be finished by the time we go in to dinner?"

Bea looked up from her sandwich.

"It'll be a little longer Alex," she said. "He has to finish fixing the other hotel first. But he'll be just a few days. Your Dad will be back before you know it, just you wait and see."

"Alex, help!" yelled Uncle Glyn. "I've lost my legs, they've been bitten clean off..."

They hadn't though, he'd just buried them in the snow.

"Can you look for 'em lad? Shoe size number nine..."

As I searched thick blobs of yellow snow started to fall from the stars. Such a thing – all that night and it was still only lunchtime! I glanced over at Aunt Bea.

"Bea? Do you remember that time when we were on the boat and looked up at the stars and there were millions of them?"

"I remember Alex..."

"That was very special wasn't it?"

"Yes, it was very special..."

"It was a very big boat..."

"Mm, very big..."

To one side of us, a big yellow blob fell like a shooting star. When it hit the beach it turned the rocks yellow too.

"The biggest boat in the world!" I was jumping up and down by now.

"Alex," said Aunt Bea. "You mustn't get so... *excited*."

"Poop poop! I'm a big boat..."

"Alex..."

"Look Aunt Bea, look! Look what's coming out of my funnel!"

On the way back Michael and I had an argument about buses. I said that the one we were on was exactly the same as the one at school, with the same seats and signs and everything. Michael didn't agree.

"It just *looks* the same," he said. "Who would take a bus all the way over to the other side?"

"But look – here's where Rhys drew a picture of a lady with two widgies..."

"It's not the same bus Alex."

"But..."

"Why would they carry a bus all the way across the sea? Do you think they don't have buses on this side?"

"I…"

"Honestly Alex, that's the stupidest thing I've ever heard…"

I looked at the lady with two widgies but didn't say anything. It was very hot on the bus. The windows were all steamed up again. 'But why would their bus be just like ours?' I thought. 'With the same scribbles and cracked window and everything?' Michael stared out at the steamed up view, even though there was absolutely nothing to see. His lips moved and he made funny little noises to himself. 'What does he know?' I thought. 'My brother, the idiot!'

When we got back to the hotel Mum had vanished again. A search party was organised, though nobody seemed that worried. "She'll turn up," said Mrs Mook. "She always does…"

She wasn't in any of the dormitories though, or the dispensary or even the hydrotherapy room. Mr Norris volunteered to go with Michael and search the garden whilst Aunt Bea and Uncle Glyn looked in the 'games-room' (I wasn't allowed to go in case I got lost myself. Growing up, I'd been lost exactly six times: twice in a supermarket, once in a chair museum, and three times on the way to school).

The truth was, ever since Dad's 'new job', Mum had been spending more and more time on her own, taking off for hours on end. No one knew where she went: one minute she was there, the next she was gone, "like the first blush of youth" (Granny Mair). "This place isn't good for her," whispered Aunt Bea. "She broods…" It was as if she were some place far from us, "in realms of her own imagining/ on some untrammelled path" (Uncle Tomos). Michael and Bea took turns spying on her, following her whenever she went off to "have a lie-down" or "look at the dark". It wasn't any use though: Mum was "inexplicable" (Auntie Glad). She needed "the close eye" (Granny Dwyn).

Instead of going straight back to our dorm, I drifted around by the bins for a time, peering in the generator room, the tennis courts, and the 'theatre' (which strangely enough had a bed in the middle of it rather than a stage). Mum wasn't there though. 'Where/oh where/ is little bear?' I sang, but then I started to feel a bit sick.

Dizzy, I went back to our 'room', my head sore and my feet leaving little blue footprints all over the tiling. I don't know what I was thinking about – Russia, maybe. What I do remember is that when I pulled back the curtain, there was Mum curled up on the bed, her legs tucked up under her but her hair spilling out *everywhere*. She wasn't asleep though. Her eyes were open but unseeing, two bright marbles in the gloom.

For a second I thought I'd wished it, not seen it, but no, it was definitely Mum, scrunched up in "the fatal position" (Cousin Louie), her eyes all shiny and black.

"Mum?"

Nothing.

"Mum? Mum, everybody's out looking for you."

No reaction.

"Shall I tell them to stop?" How foreign her face seemed! Almost like she wasn't Mum at all.

"Do you want me to fetch Aunt Bea?" I said, sidling up to "the lion's empty cage" (Cousin Gwen). "Shall I bring Uncle Glyn?"

Her face was impassive, her lips tight shut.

"Is it Michael you want me to get?"

"Michael?"

She blinked. For the first time Mum actually seemed to see me, her arm extended awkwardly in the dark.

"You're a special boy, Alex. You know that, don't you? A very special boy…"

She stroked my hair and curled the long bits back behind my ears.

"Mum?"

95

"Shhh," she said. "I love you Alex. More than anything in the world…"

"More than Michael?"

"Of course," she said smiling.

"More than Dad?"

"Of course, my love."

"More than Russia?"

How cold her hands were! Either they were very big or I was very small, 'cause they seemed to cover me entirely.

"Mum, where do you go to when you wander off? Is it to the crater? I don't like the crater. It's very slippy. I don't think you should go there. I think you should stay with us, 'cause otherwise Dad will come home from work and he won't know where you are…"

She wasn't listening though, I could tell. What was she listening to? "The mad fiddler's jig!" (Grandy).

"Mum? When do you think Dad will come back? Aunt Bea says it will be just a few days but Dr Morgan says they haven't even built the hotel yet… Mum?"

She kept on stroking me but I could tell she was someplace else, someplace far away, "across the Siberian plains…"

I fell quiet for a bit and concentrated on her hand, her scent, the sound of her breathing. The light was awful strange. Half of Mum's face was blue, the other half was black.

"Mum?" I said. "Where do you think we are? I mean, do you think they'll take us someplace else? Another hotel, maybe?"

Mum's lips were very thin, the fine white line between the sea and the horizon.

"Do you think Dad is feeling any better? Will he be there to meet us? Will everything be ready when we get there? Mum? Mum, are you okay?"

Mum's hand hovered uncertainly above me and that's when Uncle Glyn and Aunt Bea found us.

Funnily enough though, those last few days, Mum seemed, if anything, a little brighter. I mean, she went to the canteen with us, took her pills, and even played a little canasta with Aunt Bea. Michael still watched her closely though, especially when she started to cry during her last hand.

"Mikey," I said. "Do you think Mum wants to go out and slide by the bins?"

"Shh," he said. "She needs to rest."

"Do you think she'd like to play 'bomb'?"

"She doesn't want to play anything."

"But…"

"Mum needs to get her strength back. But don't let her read! And don't leave her alone…"

"But why? Isn't she well? Is she like Dad?"

Mikey pulled a funny face. "She just needs to sleep."

"Sleep?"

"She needs to let her heart calm down…"

I thought about this for a time, slowly nodding my head.

"Mikey? Do you think they'll ask Mum to go to the new hotel too?"

"No."

"I don't think Mum should get on the bus…"

"No."

"And I don't think Mum should go on her own to the crater…"

"Alex, shhh!"

The next night was the night of the fancy dress party and Mum wore a very revealing Roman toga that Michael found "indecent". I went as an out-patient (I had bandages wrapped round my head), Aunt Bea was an angel, and Uncle Glyn was Death. Michael didn't want to go because of Mum's dress but he finally agreed to come if only "to keep an eye on things". "You mean an eye on the ladies!" said

Uncle Glyn but Michael stayed "schtum".

From what I remember about that night, it was very, very busy. Hwyl was there of course, "skinny as a mouse's tail and only half the length" (Granny Dwyn). He'd come as a ghost but it was very hot inside his hood and his eye-holes weren't in the right place. "Alex?" he said. "Alex, is that you?" Mum danced with Aunt Bea and the pair of them danced with all the hairy waiters. 'My beautiful mother and my beautiful aunt,' I thought; watching them was like watching Mum dancing with a mirror. "Alex, Alex!" yelled Aunt Bea (Aunt Bea?), "Alex, come and join us!" First I danced with Aunt Bea and then I danced with Hwyl and then I danced with Mr Miskell the solicitor but after that my bandages got a little tight and I had to go and sit down to recover.

I was drinking orange juice through a straw when Mum and Aunt Bea came over, their faces awful flushed and their costumes all "awry". The pair of them were giggling like schoolgirls: that guy with the red beard! And the fella with the hairy neck! I looked at Mum and I looked at Aunt Bea and for a second I couldn't work out who was who. Ah me, I thought; if they swapped dresses then I'd be completely lost! "Are you my mummy?" I said to a woman dressed up as a nurse and Uncle Glyn laughed like a drain. Of course he was a little worse for wear by this point. "Let 'em dance," he was saying to Michael. "Is this a holiday or what?" Michael said something about the sickness but Uncle Glyn just snorted. "Well, what can you do? We're all born over open graves…"

When I turned back Mum and Aunt Bea had floated away to the dance floor, Mum's costume threatening to unravel at any moment. She was dancing with some guy in a white uniform who looked *exactly* like Able Seaman Able, but I didn't know if it was him or not; I mean, hadn't it been Aunt Bea who'd been dancing with him – and wasn't that back on the boat, before we even came to this place? The longer I watched, the more confused I got; I was about to ask Michael but then I saw the fella clap his hairy mitt on Mum's shoulder and violently lean in close. 'Little mother,' I thought, 'how big his mouth is!' The fella whispered something in Mum's ear, and Mum turned her face up towards him, her eyes closed and her mouth bent downwards. Was she crying? I turned round to look for Michael and when I turned back Mum slapped the guy full force on the cheek, the blow so strong the fella had to take two sharp steps backwards. All of a sudden there were people everywhere and I couldn't see Mum at all; instead there were dresses, dinner jackets, uniforms, all of them tangled in a big knot. My ears itched and my cheeks blushed crimson. Mummy, mummy, my beautiful mummy! The musicians kept on playing but nobody much was dancing now, everybody standing around "aghast".

Aunt Bea tried to grab Mum's hand but she was already too late; in an instance, she was across the dance floor, flinging open the patio doors and plunging head first out onto the lawn. I jumped up to follow her, but there was a chair in the way and for some reason I couldn't seem to get past it. Uncle Glyn grabbed Michael by the shoulders and roughly held him back; tch, why weren't they going after her? Didn't they care? Through the doors I could see Mum framed in her toga, her body as stiff and still as a figure on a boat. O, my frozen mummy! It was like she'd been carved and painted and nailed to the prow. 'Where are we?' I thought. 'Are we still out to sea?'

The next thing I knew Bea was standing beside her, her dress awful similar to Mum's in the strange, violet light. The two of them were framed between the snow and the sky, a kind of negative or x-ray, strange shapes on a board. How mysterious they seemed! When they came back in they both looked very cold.

"Bea?" I said. "You remember that night we saw the stars…"

"Not now Alex…"

"But…"

"Shhh!"

"It's just…"

"Not now!"

I didn't know what to say. Out in the garden, pink snow was softly falling. Meteors streaked the sky.

"Michael?" I said. "Are we in a hotel or are we on a boat?"

"I've got to go and talk to Mum…"

"I've seen that man before…"

"Alex, go and sit down!"

"His teeth are awful sharp…"

Uncle Glyn took me by the arm and led me off to one side.

"Come on Alex," he said. "You come with me…"

"His teeth!"

"It's okay Alex…"

"His mouth!"

"Alex, stop shouting…"

That night and all the next day (day?) Mum stayed in her room and read. She read all afternoon and all evening, my "melancholy momma" wrapped up in her book like a blanket. Mikey and I watched her from across the dorm; she stared at her book like she'd never stop, like she'd never do anything else ever again. Ah, what could we do? I went over to her bed and said, "Mummy, is it spring yet?" but she didn't even look up, her face pressed tight to the page. "She's… distracted," said Michael. "She's thinking about home."

Two days later she disappeared for good. Michael told me that she'd left a note but I couldn't read it because "there were too many big words". Mum had gone to look for Dad, he said, setting out on foot in the direction of the new hotel. A minibus was sent out to "see her off at the pass" (Uncle Glyn) but it came back empty. "You might as well look for a flake in a snowdrift!" (Mrs Mook). I didn't understand: why had Mum gone off on her own? And how did she know where the new hotel was being built? Aunt Bea shook her head and started to cry. "What are you crying about, there's only one road!" roared Uncle Glyn, but that only made Bea cry all the louder. "Will Dad have got a room ready for her?" I asked and Mikey said, "Alex, don't go getting any crazy ideas in your head, okay?"

While everybody else was sitting around talking I went back to our 'room' and stretched out on Mum's bed: it wasn't very warm though and didn't really smell of her. Her suitcase had gone, as had most of her things, but she'd left her Russian book behind, and her "mandatory" shoes too. What strange things to forget, I thought; hadn't she been listening when the manager had explained all about them? I pictured Mum striding across the pale blue snow, headscarf pulled tight over her face, her coat the colour of the horizon. But where was the road, the sea, the other hotel? I followed her slow hunched figure as it inched painfully across the blue, and tried to imagine the look of surprise on Dad's face as he put down his tools and saw her appear amongst the snow. What would she have brought for him – his lunch, an orange, a new pair of gloves? And what would Dad say? What's that on your feet, those aren't the right shoes, what have you done to your tights? O Mum! O Dad! O Russia! The snow blows, the air cuts like a knife and Tyurin is still not home…

4

After that Michael watched me "like a hawk". Wherever I went, he went too: playing with Hwyl, throwing snowballs at the nurses, climbing on chairs in the 'games-room'. He claimed he was my 'legal guardian'. "Who should I leave you with, Glyn and Bea? You might as well leave the cat with the cream…" The truth was, I'd already made plans to follow Mum and Dad as soon as "humanly possible". I'd hidden floppy dog, some biscuits and a knife from the canteen ("great hall!") in a plastic bag, and then stowed the whole lot under my dirty laundry. "Mikey?" I said. "Do you think the new hotel is very far?" Mikey shook his head and looked me up and down. "You're not going anywhere," he said, wagging his finger at me. "You just stay where I can see you…"

That night I had another dream about Grandy and Auntie Glad: they were still holed up "down below", but this time the hold was the next ward along, the ink spilling out from under their door and spreading out across the floor toward us. When I woke up my bed was wet and my pyjamas kind-of yellowy. Poor me! It was "too late to get the milk back in the bottle" (Granny Mair) but I got out of bed and went to look for the bath-room anyway.

Then, just as I was about to open the door, a beautiful vision materialised right in front of me: Mabel in her dressing gown, carrying her po to the loo.

"Who's there?" she yelled.

I tried hiding my wet patch but what could I do? Luckily it was pretty dark and I was only wee…

"I've had an accident," I said. "I'm a bit damp."

Mabel stared at me uncertainly in the gloom.

"Is that you Alex?"

"Mm."

"Michael's brother?"

"Mm." I moved my hand away from the damp patch. "I need to change my pyjamas," I said. "My bottoms have got a funny smell."

Mabel nodded and looked me up and down. "Oh Alex," she said. "I heard about your mummy. Are you okay? How are you all doing?"

I nodded and looked down at my stain.

"There was a wave and then I felt a little damp…"

"You must be feeling awful…"

"My legs are cold…"

"I mean…"

"My bed's wet too…"

"Um…"

Mabel moved a little closer and I could make out her pale eyes, her tangled hair, a spot appearing just above her lips. She was wearing her mum's long dressing gown and looked like she'd put her make-up on with a spoon.

"Alex?"

"Mm."

"Alex, are you listening?"

"Mm."

All at once Mabel placed her hands on my shoulders and spoke very seriously, her voice alarmingly low and husky. She was very "alluring" (Cousin Neil). "Alex, you've got to tell Michael something. Alex, are you listening Alex? Put that down then – Alex, this is very, very important. They're going to move all the kids out to schools. Anyone under sixteen will have to leave the hotel. My mum heard it from one of the cooks: because we've been here so long, the children all have to go to special schools."

"My school is across the bay," I said. "I fell off the climbing frame…"

Mabel's voice was very low and very soft.

"You've got to go and tell Michael, Alex. We're all going to have to go pretty soon. Tell him that he'll have to get ready. Alex, are you listening? They're going to move us all out of the hotel…"

Mabel really was very pretty, even with her mad hair and spot. Her face hovered in the dark like a flashlight.

"You'll tell him, Alex? You'll tell him what I said?"

"Sure," I said. "Sure I will."

"You promise? You'll tell Michael, okay?"

"Mm."

"Promise?"

"Mm."

"Okay. Night, Alex, Take care."

"Night night…"

"Don't forget now."

"Night night…"

Mabel and her dressing gown retreated into the gloom. I toddled off to the bathroom but the well was dry, no matter how hard I pumped. Tired, I went back to bed and fell into a deep, dreamless, sleep. The wet patch on my bed wasn't so bad. I soon forgot my dream about the sea and the waves. By the time I woke up my mind was as empty as a bowl.

That day's excursion was to Schröter's Valley, a good hour's journey from the hotel. Aunt Bea and Uncle Glyn said they'd go with us "to help out" and Michael nodded and told me to put on my special shoes.

The sky was really odd that morning, a deep, deep blue. It was even darker than when we'd gone to bed, darker than "a shadow's underclothes", like half the world had been cut away. The stars seemed to have gone out. A strong wind was blowing. Turquoise snow drifted across the drive and piled up against the out-buildings. "And we're going *out*?" (Aunt Bea).

Still, at least breakfast was nice. I couldn't get enough of that grey stuff ("*pottage*" – Mrs Mook) and gobbled it down by the bowl full, especially now that Mum and Dad weren't around to tell me off. I was really piling on the pounds these days, like someone had blown me up with a foot pump. Mabel kept sending Michael and me significant glances but I'd completely forgotten about our midnight rendezvous and spooned in more *pottage* instead.

Aunt Bea wasn't all that keen. "Just look at that sky," she said. "Like it's about to spill over the edge..."

"Tch, we'll be fine," said Uncle Glyn. "Fresh air is nature's cure..."

The bus was waiting for us outside – the same one as always, of course. It seemed like almost everyone from the hotel was going; Mrs Mook and Mabel, Mr Chattarji, Mrs Jenkins the chiropodist, even Dr Morgan in his dressing gown. White Star staff helped those who were a little reluctant to get on board, and by the time they'd finished every last seat was taken – "like two pints in a one-pint mug" (Cousin Jim).

With difficulty the driver pulled away from the hotel and took the road toward the 'mountains', even though they were just dirty grey smudges on the window. Every time I looked out of the window, I wondered if I'd see Mum: "Is this the yellow brick road?" I asked. The pass twisted this way and that, the bus's engine grumbling at the steep bits. Had Mum really come this way? Blobs of thick blue snow stuck to the windows. The headlights hardly seemed to work. It was as dark outside as inside your head.

"Mikey?" I said. "Is it night or is it day?"

"Well, are you awake or asleep?"

"Awake."

"It's day then."

"Okay."

The bus climbed even higher till it felt the roof might bump up against the thick black line of the sky.

"Those are probably magnificent views," said Mrs Mook. "If only you could see them…"

It felt less like climbing a mountain than entering a huge, endless tunnel. Was this the right way? I'd never been this far from the hotel before. Come to think of it, I'd never been up a mountain before. After a while I started to get a nosebleed and Aunt Bea had to plug up my nose with her scarf ("Couldn't you bring a tissue?") The bus seemed to be having problems keeping to the road; the driver kept saying rude words and Aunt Bea told me to close my ears. "But how?" Tch, what a trip it was! The engine groaned, the wipers whined and the heater gave off a smell like kids' coats left drying over a radiator.

Then we were there: at the very top of the world. We pulled into an empty car park – which is to say, a gravel clearing by a little shed on the side of a hill – and the bus slid to a halt over by a shallow ditch. Next to the shed you could make out what seemed to be a number of giant wheels set up alongside a series of cables and wires.

"We're here, we're here!" I yelled and Aunt Bea said, "Here?"

It was all very exciting. In the shed we were taken to one side and all individually weighed (I'm sorry to say that I'd filled out a bit); afterwards each of us was given a ticket and a cup of tea. "I'm seventy-two!" I told Michael, proudly. "How old are you?" Then there was just time to go to the loo before we had to queue up to get in the carriages. It was kind-of windy out there, the cars hanging from the winch like apples on a tree. "All aboard the gravy boat!" yelled Uncle Glyn. I held Aunt Bea's hand and pushed my way over to the window. Nothing below us and nothing above! Still, I managed to press myself in next to the glass, my nose reflected snout-like in the dark. "Look Mikey, I'm a piggy!" I yelled. Michael didn't say anything: he looked rather pale and hung in the middle of the car by a roof-strap. "Peel back the barf-bags!" laughed Uncle Glyn, eating a sandwich right by him.

All at once the winch started and the whole car seemed to sway rather alarmingly. There was a great deal of nervous laughter and more than a little crying. I didn't mind though; I liked being up in the air. "Look Aunt Bea," I said, "our bus looks like a toy!" "Mm," she said. "Just like my toy back home..." The car slowly rose up toward the sky and we could really feel the wind and the cold.

"Alex, don't steam up the glass little lion, I can't see out..." said Aunt Bea.

"Are we going to the top?"

"Yes, Alex."

"The very top?"

"Yes, Alex."

"But what's on top of that?" I asked but Aunt Bea was looking the other way and fiddling around in her handbag. The carriage rocked this way and that and you could hear the wind howling and screaming. Then, before I knew it, we'd reached the first observation platform and everybody had to file out. Tch, how short the trip was, how soon it was over! Luckily we were only half way up the mountain (mountain?) and the thick black cables stretched up high above us.

"Alex, where are your mittens?"

"Back in the bus..."

"And your scarf?"

"I wrapped it round floppy dog. He was cold..."

"Oh, Alex..."

It was unbelievably windy out on the platform. For a moment I thought that Dr Morgan's dressing gown might take off, but luckily a White Star guard held it down with a stick. It *was* kind of cold though: even inside my big puffer jacket I could feel my skin starting to turn blue.

"Mikey?" I said. "Is a valley at the top or the bottom?"

"The bottom."

"Then what are we doing here?"

He sighed and told me to look at the view. There didn't seem to be that much to see though. Black, black and black again. There were no lights on *anywhere.*

"Do you think we can see our house from here?" asked Mrs Mook. "I can't even see my shoes!" (Uncle Glyn).

"What about the other hotel?" asked Mrs Jones. "Any luck?"

We squinted and stared but for the life of us all we could see were black shapes and navy snow, no buildings anywhere. I had absolutely no idea where Schröter's Valley might be: behind the power lines maybe.

Aunt Bea gave my hand a squeeze and I gazed up at her. 'How lovely she is,' I thought, 'how sweet!' Apart from my mother she was the most beautiful woman in the world...

"Alex!" said Uncle Glyn. "Is that a yeti? There, just above your head..."

"Where, where?" I chanted.

"Can't you see him? Huge head, rows of teeth, enormous claws..."

I stared and stared but couldn't see anything.

"Where is he?" I yelled. "Where's he gone?"

"Glyn, leave the poor child alone," said Aunt Bea. "Are you warm enough, Alex?"

"I want to see the yeti!" I cried.

"Your uncle's just being silly Alex," said Aunt Bea.

"But I want to see the yeti!"

"Shh Alex, stop shouting, it's okay..."

To take my mind off the yeti, Aunt Bea asked if we'd like to go inside for a snack; it wasn't much of a café (out of date food, peeling walls, dirty cups) but at least the soup was warm. Uncle Glyn told a funny story about a horse and I snorted soup out of my nose. "You can't take that boy anywhere!" (Michael). Aunt Bea went off to go and look for some napkins but before she found them an official stood up and explained that only those over a certain height would be allowed to go up to the next landing: all the children would have to go back down.

Everyone looked at each other blankly.

"Just the children, you say?" said Mr Llewellyn.

Aunt Bea looked concerned.

"Glyn? I think we should go back too…"

"Hm? What do you mean?"

"Well, we can't leave them…"

"Tch, they'll be fine," said Uncle Glyn, reaching for the last piece of bread. "You'll look after Alex won't you Michael? There now, look you. Not far to go to the top now…"

"I don't think Alex would like being left on his own, would you Alex?"

"I want to go to the top!"

"There, see…"

"Psh! We won't be long, Alex. Michael'll keep an eye on you, eh? There's a good boy. It's okay Alex, we won't be long…"

"I don't think…" said Michael.

"I want to see the yeti!"

"I don't think that we should…"

"I want to see the yeti!"

"Alex, shh!"

Mabel looked like she was frantically trying to signal something to us across the way but I didn't know what.

"I want to go to the top!" I yelled.

Before I knew what was going on we all had to line up before a tape measure chalked up on one wall; anyone too small (Michael made sure he hunched his shoulders), or too young, was immediately sent to the left.

"Michael?" I said. "Why can't we go to the top?"

"Shh," he said. "You're sticking with me…"

"But I want to go with Aunt Bea and Uncle Glyn…"

"They won't be long," he said. "You're not big enough to go…"

"I am a big boy! I am a big boy!"

"Shhh…"

Two more cars were waiting for the adults; they weren't as plush as ours though, and didn't seem to have any seats.

"You make sure you wait for us at the bottom," said Aunt Bea. "Don't go wandering off, Alex. And Michael, watch your brother…"

Michael nodded and protectively put one hand on my shoulder. Up above us the cars were swinging like enormous bells. The wind was very bad.

"Come on Bea, your carriage awaits…"

Aunt Bea looked at us, looked back at Uncle Glyn, and then stepped gingerly into the car.

"We won't be long. Just don't go anywhere when you get back down…"

Uncle Glyn winked and raised his hand in a mock salute.

"Off we go boys – see you in the funny papers!"

"Michael – watch Alex!" yelled Aunt Bea.

"Bye boys! G'bye!"

I watched them go with tears in my eyes: not because I was worried but because I wanted to go too. What a con! What a swindle! I was still cross even after we'd got back into our car, watching helplessly while the adults were hoisted up into the black clouds. It looked terribly stormy. Thick grey snow was blowing sideways.

"But why can't kids go up?"

"I don't know Alex."

The cable gave a strange, drawn-out groan.

"Do you think they'll see the yeti?" I asked.

"Alex, hold onto the strap."

"Can we get more soup?"

"I said hold on to the strap."

After a few minutes our car started to go down too. It was impossible to see anything higher up the mountain; I mean, you could see the cables and the winching mechanism, but of the other cabs, nothing. Where were Aunt Bea and Uncle Glyn?

"Fly away Peter, fly away Paul," I yelled.

"Alex, be quiet," said Michael.

The car swung from side to side, making some of the smaller children cry. What was above us anyway? Higher up, the sky swallowed everything.

"Bye Aunt Bea! Bye Uncle Glyn!"

"Alex, shhh…"

The cables looked like a ladder climbing up into the sky.

"Bye cable car!" I shouted and the two of us stared out into the void. "Goodbye everybody!"

"Shh!"

When we reached the bottom, we were told we would have to wait on the bus because it was too cold to linger outside. From where I was sitting you could hardly see the cable car at all, just piles of greeny-blue snow (snow?).

"Do you think they're at the top yet?" I asked.

"I don't know Alex," said Michael.

"Do you think there is a top?"

"There's always a top…"

"But it's very dark…"

"That doesn't mean there isn't a top…"

"But…"

"Just because you can't see something doesn't mean it's not there…"

"Um," I said.

We waited for a few minutes and then the driver started the engine and the bus started to pull away. Instantly, a strange collective shiver passed through all the kids; ah us, we thought, something isn't right here…

"Where are we going?" I asked. "Aren't we waiting?"

Mikey looked grim-faced but didn't say anything.

"Weren't we told to wait at the bottom?"

No answer.

"How will the grown-ups get back?" I asked.

I couldn't work out why Michael wasn't answering me. Couldn't he hear?

"What will happen when they get back down?"

Zip. Michael was "silent as a slipper".

"Mikey?"

"Alex, quiet!"

Oddly, we didn't seem to be taking the road back to the hotel, but rather some kind of narrow track leading on through the mountains. Hwyl kept asking about his mum but the rest of the kids seemed very, very quiet.

"Michael, is this the right road?" I asked.

"It must be…" he said, but not very convincingly.

"So why aren't we waiting for the grown-ups?"

Michael seemed to be coming back round now and was looking at me with a very concerned expression on his face.

"Oh, they'll be coming on soon…" he said, holding on to my sleeve.

"But we're in the only bus, aren't we?"

"I guess it'll have to come back out," said Michael, but I didn't believe him, not even for a second. They're gone, I thought, I'll never see them again. Gone, gone, gone! Tch, my brother, the liar!

"Goodbye Aunt Bea, goodbye Uncle Glyn!" I yelled.

"Shh," hissed Michael, angrily.

As the bus edged along the track I suddenly realised we wouldn't get to see the hotel again either.

"Goodbye floppy dog, goodbye special knife," I yelled.

"Alex, will you *shut up*?"

Little mother, I thought, dear heart: how would Mum and Dad find us now?

Montes Taurus

1

"Michael?" I said. "Why aren't we going back?"

"I don't know," he whispered, watching the valley sink back into nothingness. "Maybe the snow is too deep…"

"You said it wasn't snow…"

"Well, in terms of its chemical structure, no…"

I started kicking the seat in front of me.

"Do you think we're going to the other hotel?"

"I don't know Alex. Don't go getting any funny ideas now…"

"Do you think Mum and Dad will be waiting for us?"

"I don't know, Alex."

"Michael? Do you think you should ask the driver where we're going?"

"No."

"Do you want me to ask him?"

"No."

"I will if you want me to…"

"You stay in your seat."

"But he might tell us…"

"Alex, no."

For some reason Michael was holding onto the hood of my puffer jacket, his voice strained and his eyes kind of red.

"Mikey?"

He ignored me.

"Mikey?"

"Mm?"

"Do you think they'll have bunk-beds at the other hotel?"

"I don't know, Alex."

"Can I have the top bunk if they do?"

"You can have the top bunk," he said wearily.

"Really?"

"Really."

"Thanks Michael, that's great…"

My brother, the saint!

"That's okay."

There wasn't much to see through the windows: everything was very blue. A few of the kids were crying but it was kind of hard to hear anything above the sound of the heaters. Just as I was about to ask about the driver again, a scrunched up ball of paper landed in Michael's lap. When we turned round I saw Mabel trying to signal to him from her seat towards the back, her painted eyes heavy with meaning. Mikey opened it and stood up.

"Alex, stay here, okay?"

"Where are you going?"

"I have to talk to someone."

"Is it a girl?"

"Just stay where you are."

"Can I talk to the driver?"

"No."

"Can I talk to Hwyl?"

"No."

Mikey went to the back of the bus to talk to Mabel and I was left staring out of the window like a dummy. I tried making things up again, but all I could think about was Aunt Bea and Uncle Glyn. Bea and Glyn/Bea and Glyn/Who can know/The trouble they're in? The more I thought about them the sadder I felt so I thought about something else instead. Mabel and Michael were still talking very intently at the back of the bus so I leaned across and yelled to Hwyl across the aisle.

"Hwyl?" I said. "When do you think your mummy will come back down?"

"Mummy told me to wait at the bottom," he said, rocking from side to side in his seat.

"Do you think we had to get on the bus so the cable car wouldn't fall and squash us?"

"It won't fall! Take that back! It won't fall!"

"I mean, with all that wind and all…"

"It won't! Shut up!"

"Look Hwyl, there it goes now! Wooo…"

"Is not. Take that back!"

"Boooosh," I said, making the sound of an explosion with my lips.

"You've got a stupid head," he shouted across the aisle. "I'm not talking to you…"

"Boom!"

Silence.

"Hwyl?"

He wasn't looking.

"Hwyl?"

Nothing.

"Look, I've drawn a fish on the glass. Do you want to see?"

Hwyl didn't want to talk so I went back to scuffing my shoes. They

115

were pretty dirty by now, to be honest – and these my 'special' shoes too! When I stared out of the bus it looked like the hand-trees were waving to me, shaking their little white fingers. 'Hullo,' I mouthed. 'Hullo, can you see me?' The fingers waved and pointed up at the thick black line of the sky. Hello, hello!

The next thing I knew Michael was sitting next to me again. He wouldn't say anything about what he and Mabel had been talking about though. I tried asking him but he just said, "You just stay with me, Alex," and that was that. Who knew what Mabel had said? Maybe she wanted to kiss him. Maybe she wanted to kiss me too! She sure was "a good looking piece" (Cousin Ray). I imagined her lips landing on me like a butterfly. Mabel, Mabel, willing and able! But then I fell asleep.

When I woke up the snow had turned from blue to a kind of purpley-red, but apart from that it was hard to know how long we'd all been going. My seat felt kind of uncomfortable. The window was all steamed up. When I looked over at Michael he was watching me like a prison guard.

"If we have to get out," he whispered to me. "Then don't leave my side. Do you hear me Alex? Don't go."

"Are we nearly there?"

"Alex? You stay with me – no matter what. Alex, do you hear?"

I nodded but it was hard to know what he was going on about. Sure, the bus was going a bit slower, and there were some lights in the distance, but you know, big deal: "Why the sour apples?" as Granny Dwyn used to say.

The bus made its way through some sort of gate and then rolled along a desperately uneven, slippery track. Two big square buildings, simple as one of my drawings, stood before us, separated by a high mesh fence and some kind of walkway. A few lights were on in each, but they didn't look as welcoming as our old hotel. Each had a concrete playground in front of it, and a couple of rusted swings.

"Okay Alex, no matter what the grown-ups say, you stick with me, d'you hear? Hold onto my hand…"

I looked at him funny.

"I'm not holding your hand…"

"Alex, do as you are told…"

"Hwyl will see me…"

"Alex!"

The bus was sliding to a halt now, its headlamps lighting up the fence. Mikey was talking to me but for some reason I found it awful hard to concentrate. The buildings were very square and very straight.

"Alex, are you listening?"

"Yes," I lied.

"Okay then. Do as I say…"

A few minutes later the doors opened again and some fella climbed on board, his big droopy 'tache clambering on before him.

"Now then children," he said, "listen carefully to what I'm about to tell you." He started reading out a list of who had to go to big school and who had to go to small school, but my thoughts were away with the fairies (I'd also got my hood stuck between the seat and the head-rest).

"Mikey, am I big or am I small?" I asked.

"It doesn't matter," he said, holding onto my puffer jacket. "You're staying with me…"

"Right now children, let's go," said the fella. "No hiding on the bus now…"

"Mikey?" I held onto my brother. "Michael, I don't know where to go…"

"Go where I go," he said, and with that we all had to climb down from the coach, gingerly stepping out into the queer, resiny-blue snow. The big kids were led toward one block, the little ones toward the other, and I followed Mikey, like the little goose in the story. However I'd only gone a few steps when some fella and his whiskers pounced on me and clamped a big hairy paw on my shoulder.

"Not you, little goose, not you…"

I stared desperately at Michael but other guards (teachers?) were busy frog-marching the big kids the opposite way.

"But…"

"This way wee-man. You follow me…"

I saw Mikey arguing with Mr Hairy Nose but they seemed awful far away. 'Michael!' I wanted to cry. 'Michael, come and get me!'

"Sir?" I said. "Sir, I may look like a very small boy, but really I'm not…"

The fella barely looked at me, just took hold of my hood and led me by the nose.

"Sir?"

We were getting closer and closer to the big square block.

"Sir, there's been some terrible mistake…"

I twisted my neck but – ah, me! – it was kind-of hard to see. Mikey was still talking to the fella. The snow was still blue. The other block seemed terribly far.

The next thing I knew I was through the gate and standing in the playground. For a second I felt completely lost but then I saw Hwyl standing next to me, his eyes as big as saucers.

"Alex?" he said. "Alex, why are you crying? Is it 'cause your brother had to go to the other school?"

"No."

"Did you want to go with your brother?"

"No."

Close up the school looked strangely flat, like something painted on cardboard.

"Alex?"

The door was a big black square.

"Alex? Do you think somebody will be here to collect us at home time? Alex?"

The black square opened. There was another black square inside. This square was even darker.

2

Our main teacher was Miss Bedford, a round, kindly knot of a woman, like a potato, but with glasses. She had a very low, very gentle voice, and allowed us to do whatever we liked, with the exception of skipping meals and stabbing each other with sticks. Whenever I saw her, I sang, 'Granny, granny/round and grey/knit me a hat for my wedding day' – heaven knows why. Miss Bedford had a single grey hair hanging down from the end of her chin, which I was drawn to like a magnet. Up close it resembled an emergency cord, or a rope you might ring for dinner – tch, I couldn't keep my eyes off it. Ah, poor Miss Bedford, saddest of all my teachers! If it wasn't for that hair she'd have disappeared from my memory entirely...

My favourite lesson was painting. The brushes were terribly old and stuck together, but I didn't really mind: I did big blobby paintings, dabbing on crude splodges of snow in whatever colour I could reach on the paint table. My pictures were all pretty much the same: big black squares (which is to say, houses), covered by hundreds of daubs of thick, sticky paint (snow), the occasional stick figure hiding somewhere near to the heavy black line of the ground. When I was finished, I would take the sopping wet piece of paper (I always put too much paint on my brush) and leave it to dry on one of the enormous radiators that lined the room. A few hours later it was all crinkled and brown and gave off a strange aroma, and then I would carefully place it on my desk and think about it. When it dried it smelled like sick.

Apart from painting there were sums (boring!), writing (hard) and 'physical co-ordination', which seemed to involve walking round and round the room. We were hardly ever allowed outside, and even if we were, this squat little fella with hairy ears – Mr Carver – had to come with us, watching us like we were "the last beans on his plate" (Grandy). From the playground you could look across at the big school but apart from a light on in one of the high windows, you couldn't really see anything – well, not Michael, anyway. For some reason the big kids weren't allowed out the same time as us, so even at break time the great block stayed silent. In fact I wasn't even sure if the older children were allowed out at all: I mean, there weren't any footprints on the other side of the fence, and you never heard a bell or anything. I tried asking Miss Bedford about 'big school' but all she'd say was, "Why are you in such a hurry to grow up?" and ruffle my hair. Oh, Brother Michael! I felt very alone and very small. From our block, the other square looked terribly black and flat. It was hard to imagine it had an inside at all.

All the little kids – and there were about twelve of us – slept in a big, long hall that had been turned into a dormitory. The beds were exactly the same as the ones in the hotel: all the sheets and pillowcases had 'property of White Star Shipping' printed on them too. We were given little blue uniforms, knitted bobble-hats and slippers to be worn indoors; outside you had to put on your special shoes of course. The dorm was pretty grim. We had a khaki duvet, a khaki throw, and a peg for our coat. Above my peg was the name 'Susan' but I didn't say anything. We were also handed a box to put our 'things' in, even though our 'things' were back at the hotel. I missed my comics, my soldiers, floppy dog. The youngest amongst us, Mabdwen, was given a toy panda but it only had one eye and smelled of wee. He looked at it suspiciously and so did I. Who knew where it came from? The panda had a very strange nose. It also had very strange ears. Come to think of it, it might not have been a panda at all.

The best thing about the school was the food: the same sludgy goo as before. I'd been eating it so long now I couldn't get enough of it. I was really plumping up by now; putting on my trousers was like trying to dress a football with a sock. At mealtimes I always sat next to Hwyl, 'cause he didn't want to eat anything and I could "fill my boots" (Cousin Carl) from Hwyl's plate.

"Don't you want it Hwyl? It's lovely…"

"It makes my tummy hurt…"

"Hwyl! Hwyl! Look at me! I'm a cement mixer…"

"Alex…"

"Here comes the digger…"

Meals were taken in a big draughty silo full of metal drums: whether that was where they got the grey stuff from, I don't know. It wasn't very formal. We didn't have a dinner-lady or anything, just Mr Carver in a tabard. There weren't many kids so mealtimes didn't take long. Dessert was grey stuff covered in custard. That was nice too.

The worst thing about school was when they switched off the lights at night (if it was 'night': outside the school it was just as black as outside the hotel – maybe even more so). Lying there in the gloom, the darkness seemed to seep in through the draughty windows and drip down on my bed. It was very thick. All you could hear was the sound of a generator humming and the occasional sob from one of the tots. Every night I dreamed of Grandy but in the morning (morning?) he was gone. Hwyl said that he dreamed of being on a cable car with his mum but I didn't say anything. Hwyl didn't look well. He had trouble getting out of bed and his eyes looked like two boiled eggs.

Of all the other children – Josh, Sam, Kieran and his trousers – my favourite was Milly and her kind face. Milly (or was it Tilly?) answered every question by waving her hand like a flower in a high wind. I was least keen on Amelia who squealed a lot and had very sticky palms – Josh said that she was as "nutty as a squirrel's shit", and the boys all gave her a very wide berth.

When we first arrived I wondered if Bethan would be there, but she must have been sent to somewhere else – the other hotel, maybe. Every night I lay on my bed and waited for Michael to come and get me. It was all I could think about: closing my eyes I waited for a hand on my bedclothes, Michael standing over me with a rope, or maybe a torch. It never happened though. Without any light each day was just the same. Black shutters on a black window! "Is this today or still yesterday?" I asked Miss Bedford but she told me to put my hand down and concentrate on my sums.

Surprisingly it was Wade – one of the quietest kids in the class – who was the first one to run away. I don't know what happened: one minute he was standing by the swings with the rest of us, the next he was away through the gate and taking off across the snow like a rocket. It was Hairy Mr Carver who brought him back. Wade had funny bite-marks on his neck and didn't want to talk about it. That night I heard him in his bed, crying and talking to himself. Poor Wade! I looked at the red marks on his body and shivered. In the morning Kieran and I pretended to be dinosaurs.

"Rrrrr!" I said. "I'm going to eat you up!"

"Wade is a very fast runner," said Kieran, thoughtfully. "The next time he runs away, do you think he would take us with him?"

"Grrr," I said, "I'm a big dinosaur…"

"I wish I could run like that…"

"Kieran, look at my big teeth…"

"Alex? I think I'm going to go have a lay down now."

"Rrrrr!" I said, stamping on our little town.

The next day we all had to report to the big hall for 'tests'. When we got there we were made to strip down to our vest and pants (both boys and girls) and then had all sorts of needles jabbed into us, whether we wanted them or not. Afterwards we had to blow down various tubes; my score was rubbish, but not half as bad as Hwyl's – he looked like he was "taking measurements for a winding-sheet" (Granny Dwyn).

Afterwards lessons were cancelled and we were allowed to go outside for a bit. I played 'count to one hundred' with Big Julie but just as I got to seventy-three I saw two of the nurses pushing a trolley, followed by Mr Carver, Mr Carver's hairy ears, and Dr Tweedle from the ship (ferry!). The doctor looked exactly the same as before: big black eyes, thick, cascading beard, huge, cavernous mouth. His tongue licked at a little ball of spit curled up by his jaws.

I wanted to ask Dr Twiddle what had happened to everybody else from the boat but instead I hung back by the chemical waste bin, "planning". Where were they going to anyway? The nurses pushed the trolley across the snow over to the connecting gate that led to 'big school' and keeping one eye on the doctor and one eye on Mr Carver (tch, if only I had more eyes!) I followed them over to the gate, squeezing myself flatter than a shadow. Clever Alex! While the nurses were busy with the lock, I ducked down and hid behind the trolley; it was full of files and boxes, the boxes making a little jingly noise as the nurses pushed it through the snow. Scuttling crab-like alongside it, I inched my way across the yard, which was when the doctor leaned down to talk to me.

"So then, lad, how are we?"

"I'm feeling a bit better, sir," I said, still crouching by the trolley.

"No more dizziness, faintness, feeling sick?"

"No sir."

I felt a little awkward squatting there and stood up.

"There's a good boy. And you're finishing your plate, yes? Eating everything up?"

"I like the grey stuff, sir."

"Excellent! Excellent! Well, back you go then, run along now," and with his great hairy mitt he sent me back toward the gate and little school.

Hwyl was waiting for me, along with Kieran and his trousers.

"Where have you been?" he asked.

"Big School."

"Big School?"

"Mm," I said, modestly.

"What's it like?"

"It's okay."

"Did you see your brother? Are there any other grown-ups in there?"

"Rrrr, I'm a dinosaur!" I said.

"Did the doctor say anything?" asked Kieran.

"I'm going to gobble you up!"

Then the kids all started to wander away.

That afternoon it was sums again and I drew my favourite numbers in my graph book and made up names for them. From where I was sitting I could see big red nips on Wade's arms and neck.

"Miss?" said Hwyl. "Miss, I don't feel very well. Can I go to the nurse's room?"

"Of course you can, Hwyl."

My arm immediately shot up.

"Can I go with him?" I yelled. "I mean, to help."

"Alright Alex, off you go. But you come straight back afterwards. Do you hear me Alex?"

"It's alright Hwyl," I said. "I'll look after you…"

Actually, Hwyl really didn't look so good. He had big black rings around his eyes and walked with a definite limp. Poor little fella! His movements seemed terribly slow and his head lolled from side to side like a broken doll. My plan was to run away, climb the fence, and break into big school next door, but since Hwyl did look sort of poorly, we went and sat in the nurse's room instead.

It was a little green cubicle smelling of chemicals, disinfectant and sick. The nurse wasn't there so we both climbed onto the bed and made a kind of cave. Hwyl said it was very hot inside the cave but I said there were wolves outside and he couldn't come out till I said.

"But I'm hot!" he complained.

"Shh," I said. "The wolves will hear you…"

I watched Hwyl's little lump for a while but he kept squirming and after a while I had to let him out. His face looked very red.

"Hwyl?" I said. "I think you'd better lie down…"

Where was the nurse anyway? I opened and closed the curtain around Hwyl as if putting on a show but then one of the runners got stuck so I had to stop. There wasn't much to do in the cubicle. I started flicking the lights on and off but Hwyl said it made him feel dizzy and so we tried jumping from the stool onto the bed instead.

"Aarrrgh," I yelled, as if I'd just been shot.

Afterwards we started going through all the cupboards and drawers, and fished out bottle after bottle of pills. "This one makes you better and this one turns you blue!" we sang, but unfortunately we couldn't get the tops off. Bored, we stared out of the window instead. Big dabs of greeny-blue snow were dripping down from the sky, wet little splodges in front of a black background. The glass seemed strangely distorted and it was hard to tell if the snow was falling up or down. What a strange picture it was! When I leant over and licked the window, I got little bits all over my tongue.

"Hwyl?" I said. "Hwyl, look at my tongue…"

We seemed to have been in the cubicle a long time. There still wasn't any nurse. I wondered whether we ought to go back to the classroom but when I turned round Hwyl had fallen asleep on the bed. What a funny little kid! His hair was all stuck to his head and his lips were very pale. To be honest, I felt a bit groggy too. The smell of medicine in the nurse's room was awful strong, a bit like cough medicine and a bit like glue. I bent down and licked my knees: they no longer tasted of the sea but seemed kind-of chemically instead. Not knowing what else to do, I lay down next to Hwyl and pushed my face into the bed, inhaling deeply. The khaki bedclothes were a little scratchy. The sheets reeked of chemicals too. When I closed my eyes tiny blobs and daubs floated up out of the dark, a little like the paintings I did in art class, and a little like clouds or stars too. The blobs circled each other and then drifted further and further apart, turning into little swirls as they went. Then I went to sleep too.

It was Milly-or-Tilly who found us.

"Alex?" she said. "Alex, Miss Bedford is looking for you..."

I looked up at Milly-cum-Tilly's kind, trusting eyes and said, "Mm?"

"Miss Bedford told you to come straight back..."

I nodded and looked straight at her pretty, shiny face.

"Milly?" I said. "Milly, Hwyl's dead."

Immediately Milly (or Tilly) burst into tears and started to scream.

By the time Miss Bedford arrived, Hwyl was crying too.

"I'm not dead," he sobbed. "Take it back, Alex, I'm not dead, I'm not..."

Miss Bedford, Milly, and Mr Carver all stared at me.

"He was dead, but he got better," I said.

Miss Bedford's normally mild gaze seemed to darken and I concentrated on the hair hanging down from her chin.

"I'm not dead, I'm not!" cried Hwyl.

I made my eyes as big and innocent as I could. My lips twitched into a big, babyish smile. Hwyl was still crying.

"Alex? Alex? I'm not..."

3

The next time Wade escaped was in the middle of the night. In the morning his bed was empty and his special shoes were gone. A search party was sent out to look for him whilst the rest of us sat in the canteen eating porridge ("Mm, this one's just right!") but later we saw Mr Carver stride across the yard empty-handed, turquoise snow sticking to his ears.

Dizzy Izzy said she'd seen Wade crawling out of a window when she went for a drink in the middle of the night. "And the water tasted funny too!" Milly-cum-Tilly offered to help with the search, but Miss Bedford told her to put her hand down and go and take Little Ann to the girls' toilet instead. "Every body/big and wee/has to poo/and has to pee!" (Cousin Rhodri). All the time this was going on I was thinking about Mum: why was it that some people disappeared and others didn't? I had to sit down to work it out – "a thing like this you can't decide on one foot" (Granny Mair). It's hard to imagine people being someplace else when you have to stay in the same spot all the time. Where do they go? How do they get there? Where now?

That day it was too wet to play and we weren't allowed out. Amelia wanted to play stamping but I wasn't very keen. To be honest, Amelia was a little strange; she kept clapping and jiggling and making funny squealing noises and when Josh asked if she was my sister I said no and went off to play somewhere else.

If you climbed on the radiator next to Miss Bedford's cupboard then you could look out at big school across the way. There wasn't much to see though: no shapes in the windows, no shadows under the lights, not even any footprints in the snow. It's true! The big school looked more like a cardboard cut-out than a real place. I kept hoping I'd spot one of the big kids walking out to the swings – it didn't have to be Michael or Mabel, it could have been anyone – but there was nothing, nothing but greeny snow. Did Miss Bedford teach the other kids as well or did they have a big teacher? Once in a while Mr Carver took his hairy ears over there but he soon came back. What about the older kids – did they have 'tests' too? What happened if you failed them? I wanted to keep watching but after a while the radiator started to boil my bottom and I had to climb back down.

Sitting at the table, a feeling of terrible weariness came over me. My chair, the makeshift desks, Miss Bedford's wipe-down board: all of these, for some reason, seemed unbearably, immeasurably sad.

"Michael," I mouthed. "Mikey, where are you?" but then I spotted Milly staring at me from the table opposite so I quickly looked away and stared down at my page.

"Alex?" she asked. "Alex, what is it?"

Her expression was so sweet I thought I might burst into tears right there and then.

"I've lost my toys," I said. "They're back at the hotel…"

Milly (or Tilly) looked thoughtful.

"I'm sure they're okay," she said. "They'll be right where you left them. Your mum and dad will make sure…"

I nodded and started drawing big black scribbles on my page.

"We'll all be going back soon. Going home, I mean…"

My scribbles grew bigger and bigger.

"Do you think it's still there?"

"There?"

A little cloud crossed her bright clean face.

"The other side, I mean…"

"Of course it's still there Alex," she said, looking at me strangely.

"Where else would it be?"

I didn't know. I didn't know anything. When I looked down at my scribbles I found they'd formed a big black hole. Then Milly went off to play.

There weren't any more lessons that day because of the search, so we were sent off to go and "entertain ourselves". I spent most of the afternoon scribbling: sometimes in my book, sometimes on the desk, sometimes on my arm. Outside it was snowing green.

When the bell rang we all trooped off to the main hall for porridge: this time it wasn't served by Mr Carver, but by some fella with a red mustachio I'd never seen before. He had amazingly long eyelashes and these were red too. Tch, what a funny looking fella! I was so flustered, I only asked for one portion of 'grey'.

We all shovelled down our food but everyone seemed a little quiet and distracted, like some kind of heavy weight was hanging over us. When we went back to the dorm, Wade was sitting on his bed reading a comic. The red fella immediately went to find Miss Bedford and Miss Bedford went to find Mr Carver and all the time Wade was sitting there flicking through his comic, "blithe as a bumble bee" (Mum).

When he got there Mr Carver shouted at him for a while before he was marched away to the staff-room. After about an hour or so he was back though, and we all watched as he toddled back into our dorm and climbed into bed. His brow was a bit sweaty and his cheeks seemed all aglow, but that was it.

"Wade, where did you go?"

"What did you see Wade? Did you see Mummy and Daddy?"

"Wade, what's out there? How far can you go?"

At first he just turned over and pretended to be asleep, but eventually Kieran climbed out of bed and gave his lump a quick shake.

"Wade, Wade, tell us! What happened? Where did you go?"

Wade's voice seemed to float towards us from some far off place.

"Big School."

"Big school?"

We didn't know whether to be amazed or disappointed; all that time and he'd only gone so far!

"Mm," he said, kind of sleepily.

"And what did you see?"

"It was pretty quiet. Most of it seemed all shut up. There was a store room with lots of boxes in it."

"And the big kids? Did you see them?"

"No. I couldn't really get in. Most of it was locked."

We all went quiet, taking this in. Wade's voice sounded very away as if his bed were already floating off into the darkness.

"Wade?" I asked. "Wade, will you take us?"

"Take you?"

"To Big School."

The darkness seemed immense, as high and wide as space itself.

We all waited.

"Wade?"

Nothing.

"Wade?"

The very room seemed to breathe in.

"Wade?"

"Okay."

We all stared at Wade but he seemed to be asleep.

"Big school…" I said stupidly.

After a brief discussion it was decided we should all go there the following night. Only Little Ann didn't want to go, so Milly or Tilly said she'd stay with her, 'cause it wasn't nice to be left all alone in the dark. We were a bit worried about Amelia coming because of her funny noises but she said she'd tell Miss Bedford if we left her behind so we had no choice but to "count her in".

Wadey Wade/lean and thin/open the door/and let us in! Ah, who would have guessed that so quiet a kid would turn out to know the right way across? I closed my eyes and could see little blobs floating down in the darkness. If I squeezed even tighter they seemed to change colour. The night seemed to stretch on forever. Little blobs kept on falling.

The next day went by in an excited blur. Nobody could concentrate. Even Milly-or-Tilly put her hand up at the wrong time and I couldn't get even the simplest question right.

"Alex, what's wrong with you? Do you need the bathroom?"

"No, sir."

Miss Bedford scratched her chin.

"What is it Alex? What are you looking at?"

"Nothing…"

After 'sums' it was 'physical co-ordination' in the hall. Mr Carver watched us "like a fox watches chickens" (Granny Dwyn). We had to touch our toes and do forward rolls and everything. I could barely even see my feet and Big Julie was even worse: she was plump as a dumpling and didn't so much roll as topple.

Would there be much climbing involved in getting into the big school? I wasn't so good at climbing ropes – or scrambling up walls for that matter. Then Mr Carver shouted at me and I had to go to the bathroom.

At dinnertime we were all given extra portions, but I couldn't even finish the first helping. A swarm of angry bees seemed to be buzzing inside my head. Not looking what I was doing, I spooned a big lump of gruel into my lap.

From behind the counter Mr Carver looked at me suspiciously.

"Not hungry Alex? Are you feeling alright?"

"Yes sir."

"Do you want to go to the nurse?"

"No sir."

When I glanced down at my crotch it was all grey.

"Well, eat up your supplement then."

"Yes sir."

When he'd gone I poured the whole lot on the floor.

Later that night we were woken by Wade. "Shh," he said. "Not a word." The dorm was terribly dark but Wade told us not to put any lights on. We were all a little scared. Mabdwen was crying and we agreed that he should stay with Milly and Little Ann. The rest of us put on our special shoes and moved stealthily toward the door. Apart from Mabdwen crying, I couldn't hear a thing.

In the girls' toilet you had to put one foot on the bowl, one foot on the cistern, and then haul yourself up through the window. My foot went straight in the pan and I thought, 'Oh my special shoes!' Fortunately Kieran pulled me up, squeezing me through like a button through a buttonhole. Our shoes made big ugly footprints across the yard but Wade said not to worry 'cause "our tracks" would be covered by the morning. Above us, the sky was pulled taut like a tent. A single security light illuminated the high gate. In the strange light the shadows looked like the bars of a cage.

Crocodile-fashion, we made our way along the fence to some kind of pre-fab garage or out-house about half way between the two schools. It looked very rickety, as if the merest puff would blow it over, and I remember thinking, 'Oh, if only I hadn't eaten so much porridge!' Then Wade put one foot on the windowsill, felt for the guttering, and pulled himself up. I had to be dragged up by Big Julie and Kieran. When we were all on the roof, the sky seemed very close. I put one hand up, but – nothing. Then I saw Kieran looking at me so I stopped.

Getting down from the pre-fab was actually easier than climbing up; there was a line of metal drums and some kind of skip you could balance on the edge of. It seemed to me that the snow (snow?) on the other side was a slightly different colour than ours: more yellowy, maybe. The climbing frames were exactly the same colour and didn't look like they'd been used at all.

Wade set off across the way and we stuck to him "like jam sticks to bread" (Dad? Uncle Glyn? Grandy?). Close up, 'Big School' seemed a little less flat, more like a big square block. There was a bright red security light right above the main entrance but we headed round the back way (assuming it *was* the back), crouching down whenever we came to one of the big square windows. There were no lights on though. Were Michael and all the big kids sleeping? I listened hard but all I could hear was Hwyl breathing in my ear.

"I'm tired," he said. "Alex? I want to go…"

Wade was busy testing the doors whilst Kieran and his trousers kept watch. Amelia was making popping noises by blowing on her arm.

"Here!" said Wade.

The first time he'd crawled in through a service hatch but on the way back he'd propped a door open with a bin bag. Now we all trooped in.

This was the supply room Wade had been in last time; it was full of boxes and crates and smelled like the infirmary. Wade cheerfully switched on the main light and started moving things around. The box Hwyl and I opened was full of dressings and gauze, whilst the one Kieran and Wade attacked seemed to be packed with plastic folders. Hwyl said that he didn't think we ought to break anything but was swiftly out-voted: I started stamping on all the syringes and Sam threw a roll of bandages at Josh's head.

After one particularly loud crash we all went quiet. No one came to find us though. Wade tried all the other doors but they were all locked. Hwyl had a syringe stuck in his leg. I felt a little sick.

"I think we should go back," said Hwyl.

But where should we go? On this side of the fence there was

nothing to stop you walking all the way out down to the main road but nobody was brave enough to suggest it. Instead we wandered round the playground for a bit, occasionally stopping to check the walls for "weaknesses".

"Let's split up," said Wade. "If you find a way inside, then whistle."

"Wade!" we yelled, but he didn't answer. He was gone like the "blink of a blackbird's eye" (Granny Mair). "Wade!" Nothing. "Wade!"

Amelia said she was going back. Big Julie started throwing stones at the windows. Hwyl and I went off to play 'The Farmer And His Gun'. Hwyl looked a little frightened though. "Alex?" he said. "Do you know how to whistle?"

"I'll be the farmer and you be the rabbit!" I yelled.

We made our way along a tall black wall avoiding the big drifts of green and yellow. It was a little sticky in places and awful hard to forge a path.

"Let's make an igloo," I said, pointing to a big pile of yellow snow.

The snow wasn't really the right consistency though and it turned our hands yellow too. The only thing we could make was a kind of hole, which we called "the den".

We sat inside and looked back through the bars at 'Little School'. It too looked like a big square block. Was it my imagination, or was the sky a little more grey and a little less black? It was very hard to tell. The space above us seemed to be filled with a kind of dense black fog.

"Alex?" said Hwyl. "Do you think we're a long way from the cable cars?"

"I think so," I said. "Miles and miles and miles."

"Do you think my mummy is looking for me?"

"Maybe," I said cautiously.

"Do you think your mummy is looking for you?"

"She's with Dad in the other hotel. They've probably finished making it by now."

A big yellow drip landed on Hwyl's head. We fell silent.

"Was that a whistle?" Hwyl asked.

"What?"

"That!"

I listened hard but couldn't hear anything; the night seemed very deep.

Hwyl poked his head out and looked around.

"I think that was a whistle," he said. "Do you think we should go?"

"Mm," I said, though I quite liked it in our den. It was snug and yellowy and made me feel safe. But we went out anyway.

When we climbed out we couldn't see any of the other little kids anywhere. We wandered all the way round the block but it was "empty as a poor man's pocket" (Uncle Tomos).

"Do you think I should shout 'Wade'?" asked Hwyl.

"Okay."

"Wade!"

"Wade!"

We were both a little cold by now. Our puffer jackets were stained blue and yellow. Our shoes didn't look too clever either.

"Maybe they've gone back," said Hwyl.

"Maybe…" I said.

"Shall we go back?"

"Okay."

We retraced our steps back to the little pre-fab shed but as soon as we got there we realised we wouldn't be able to climb back up the drums from this direction.

"I can't reach!" said Hwyl, crying.

"But Wade must have got back up…" I said.

"My arms are too little!"

I looked at the drums, and then at the skip.

"We'll have to go back to big school and wait for the big kids to get up," I said.

Hwyl looked at me despondently but I said, "The big kids, Hwyl!

We'll finally get to see them! That okay, Hwyl? The big kids?"

Hwyl looked uncertain, but I was "ecstatic" (Michael). Finally, I'd get to see what they did at 'Big School' – whether it was lessons or games or something else entirely.

We trudged back toward the building discussing whether to go break in through a window or simply walk up to the main entrance instead. We were both a bit tired by now. Hwyl had a yellow head.

"What if we just knock?" I asked.

Inside was a tiny lobby, all in darkness, with some kind of reception desk and a few chairs scattered around. It seemed kind-of abandoned and surprisingly small. It didn't look like a school at all.

We walked across the lobby and one of us (me? Hwyl?) managed to switch on a light. We could see better now but that didn't make it any more interesting.

The next room along was a dormitory, not unlike the one back in little school. It was pretty empty though. We went through into a second dormitory and that turned out to be deserted too. It was all very boring. The khaki sheets and little lockers were just like ours but something about the room made me think of the sickbay where I'd spotted Grandy and Auntie Glad. It had a strange below-decks feel to it. At times it felt like this room was swaying from side to side too.

"Alex?" said Hwyl. "I don't think there are any big kids here…"

I didn't say anything.

"I don't think this is a school at all, what do you think? Alex? Alex?"

I didn't know what I thought. Instead I tried lying down on one of the beds.

"Alex, are you tired?"

Truth be told, I was thinking about Michael. He'd told me to stick to him "like glue" but somehow I'd managed to lose him anyway. Ah, what had really happened here? Had the bus taken everyone away without us noticing? Or hadn't the big kids ever been here at all?

Lying on the bed I could look out of one of the windows and gaze back at 'Little School'. I idly wondered whether Wade and the other kids had gone back, or if any of the grown-ups – Miss Bedford or Mr Carver or even that fella with the red brush – had even noticed we'd gone. To be honest, I felt too tired to care. My limbs felt terribly heavy. My nose was wet. My shoes were covered in paint. I no longer wanted to move.

"Alex?" said Hwyl. "Alex, we'd better go…"

I pretended to be asleep.

"Alex?"

Across the way Milly (or Tilly) and Little Ann and Mabdwen and Mabdwen's panda would all be tucked up in bed, Amelia would be making weird popping noises with her arm, Kieran would be hanging up his trousers. And yet none of that seemed real somehow… No, when you were in a different place to someone, the place that they were didn't seem quite real – more like something in a book or a picture or just a shape in the fog…

"Alex? Alex, are you asleep?"

I stared at the strange flat square and tried to imagine how they could be there whilst Hwyl and I were here. It didn't make sense, somehow. I mean, was there a 'here' and a 'there' in the first place? What did 'here' and 'there' mean anyway? But then my head started to hurt so I turned to see what Hwyl wanted instead.

"Alex? Alex, I can hear something…"

I listened hard.

"Hwyl?"

"Shh! There! There Alex, there!"

And then I heard it too.

4

Something – or somebody – was moving about in the darkness. I tried to work out how far away it was but it was awful hard to tell. It was like a heavy shoe, or maybe a series of soft thuds. Hwyl and I looked at each other and blinked hard.

"Do you think it's a big kid?" asked Hwyl.

"Let's turn the light off," I said.

Hwyl ran over to the switch and everything went black. My heart was beating pretty fast. I slid down under the bed, as the sound of movement grew closer. What was it anyway? More like a pad than a step.

"Hwyl?" I whispered.

The darkness seemed endless.

"Hwyl?"

"What?" he hissed.

"Is that you?"

"Yes…"

"Really?"

"Yes."

"Where are you?"

"Over here."

"Where?"

"Over here, by the door…"

"What, is that you?"

"Alex, shh!"

And then I saw it: a glimpse of hair, or maybe whiskers, or maybe even some kind of fur. A picture of an animal suddenly flashed before my eyes – something I'd seen on a card at school maybe, or perhaps in a book.

"Wolves!" I screamed.

Hwyl made a bolt for the door and I was right behind him, yelling "Wolves! Wolves! Run Hwyl, run!"

The two of us sprinted clean across the second dormitory and back out into the lobby, Hwyl crying and me shouting, "Wolves, Hwyl, wolves right behind us!"

The thing was, the more I said it, the more I believed it too. I could almost see the hounds right behind us, their red eyes, wide jaws, the wolves' sharp glistening teeth…

Hwyl seemed to stumble and I imagined the wolves falling on him, gobbling him all up. It didn't happen though. Instead we kept on running.

"Wolves! Wolves!" we both shouted.

We reached the main doors and ran "hell for leather" toward the snow. In my mind a great cloud of teeth snapped ravenously at our heels, an enormous avalanche of fur and claws and bad breath…

"Alex!" yelled Hwyl. "Where are they?"

"Keep running!" I said. We hurtled down the drive and out toward the road, heading in the direction of more of those finger-trees, even though they were kind-of spindly and not much use. The trees, the trees! Then I stopped to tie my laces and Hwyl stopped with me.

"Have they gone?" he asked, a streak of snot trailing down onto his puffer jacket.

"I think so…" I said.

"Did you see them?"

I nodded.

"Wolves?"

I nodded again and tried doing up my laces, though it's hard to do when you've got a stitch.

"Alex, what were wolves doing in Big School?"

I shrugged. "Maybe they use them as guard dogs or…"

Hwyl looked at me intensely. "Or?"

"Or maybe…"

"Maybe what?"

"Rrrr," I said, baring my teeth.

"Alex, don't scare me…"

"Rrr…"

"Alex, I'm going to tell a teacher…" Hwyl turned around and started marching back toward the two schools.

"Hwyl!" I cried out. "Hwyl, you can't go back…"

He stopped and stared at me.

"Why not?"

I tried to think. I still had my arms stretched out in a very scary way.

"We can't go back. Not now we've broken into Big School and smashed up all the boxes and woken up the dogs…"

Hwyl paused to consider this, sending an anxious glance in the direction of the black square and the big fence.

"But we've got to go back," he said, sounding near tears again. "I'm tired and I'm hungry and I want to go to back to my bed…"

I licked my lips and tried to sound grown-up. Hwyl looked very scared.

"Hwyl, we can't. We'll get told off. We won't get any more 'grey'. The wolves will eat us all up."

Poor Hwyl looked lost, unable to take a step in either direction. His little mouth trembled and a string of snot stretched from his nose to the top of his zip. What a funny little tick! Skinny as a worm's tie…

"C'mon Hwyl," I said, a little more gently. "We'll go find the cable cars and then we'll go and find your mum. Maybe it isn't so far. We should be there by morning – what do you say? Maybe we can walk to the other hotel…"

Hwyl looked at me uncertainly.

"The other hotel will be a lot nicer. There'll be food and warm beds and a swimming pool and everything. C'mon Hwyl. It can't be far…"

Shaking his head Hwyl wandered back over to me, his little puffer jacket shaking.

"Are you sure my mum will be there?"

"Where else?"

We started making our way between the trees, trudging between the piles of yellow-green snow.

"Do you think we'll be there by breakfast?"

"It's probably just through these trees…"

"And you know the way?" Hwyl said, suspiciously.

"The way? Sure – my big brother Michael told me, Michael the explorer…"

Behind us I could hear something sniffing the air and pausing to paw the ground, but I didn't dare say anything. Black paint congealed around us. The trees dripped. It was still night.

From Tycho's Crater to The Straight Wall

1

Hwyl and I walked between the thin white trees, our 'special' shoes growing heavier by the foot. The trees were very tall and very bare. Hwyl was limping and my laces were undone on both feet.

"Alex?" said Hwyl. "Alex, didn't we come along a big road – in the bus, I mean? Alex?"

"Shhh!" I said. "You'll wake the bears…"

The snow was pretty deep and our feet made funny little plopping sounds as we made our way through it. After a while we came to a beck full of a purplish liquid – melt-water? Gesso? – and we followed it for a while, taking care not to slip on the slippery paste.

"D'you think we should drink it?" I asked, but Hwyl looked suspicious. He seemed very tired – like "a flea with a dog on its back" (Granny Dwyn). He didn't even want to play 'up to one hundred'.

"What's wrong?" I said. "Not thirsty?"

To be honest, Hwyl seemed to be going slower and slower. Most of the time, the ground was really uneven, full of little holes and bumps. The finger-trees were very close together. From down below they looked like sign posts with the words scored out. Hwyl looked sad. "My shoes are all spoilt," he cried. "It's alright," I said, "it's only blue…"

Above us the fog was thinning a little and I could see the big black line at the top of the sky. After that – who knew? Stars? Planets? Maybe if we took our shoes off we'd float straight up, all the way to heaven. How far was it to heaven anyway? "Further than a cat can jump!" (Dad). "Alex?" said Hwyl. "I think I might have to stop for a little bit…" He gazed at me with big puppy eyes but I didn't listen. The path (path?) started to climb upwards and after a while I started making engine noises and puffing like a stream train. There were thick clumps of blue, followed by little spills of red. Once in a while I thought I heard the wolf following us but I didn't say anything. Looking back, Hwyl looked a little 'distressed'.

"My feet hurt," he said.

"Maybe it's your special shoes. Do you want to take them off?"

"No."

"Do you want to eat some blue?"

"No."

"Do you want to drink some red?"

"I want to sit down…"

I made a funny popping sound with my mouth.

"Maybe from the top we'll be able to see the cable car place. Or the valley…"

"I've got a stitch…"

"Maybe we can even see the sea … or the way back to our side…"

"Our side?" asked Hwyl.

"Our side!" I sang. "Our side, our side, our side!"

Hwyl didn't say anything.

"What do you think has happened to all our things?" I asked. "Do you think they're safe?"

Silence.

"Do you think anyone would break in whilst we're away?"

Nothing.

"Do you think our houses are still there or do you think they've moved?"

Still no response.

"Hwyl?"

When I glanced back at him Hwyl looked kind-of poorly so I concentrated on getting myself up the hill instead. The blue was very deep.

There was a sort-of track here, but it was awful hard to make it out under all the snow. It's funny, you would have thought that it would have been terribly cold, but that's not how I remember it. Maybe it was our jackets keeping us warm, or maybe it was the effort of climbing up the big bank, but I felt kind of sweaty, truth be told. My head itched and my nose burned. Every once in a while I caught sight of something big and hairy following us through the trees, but I didn't say anything – "why scare the cook?" (Granny Mair). The main thing was that that thing was there and we were here. Whatever it was, it was keeping its distance, waiting for us to slow down or maybe fall asleep.

"What is it?" asked Hwyl.

"I'm counting trees," I said.

"Mm."

"Do you want to know what I'm up to?"

"Mm."

Hwyl was a funny looking kid, skinny as a cat's whisker, with big saucer eyes and a little round mouth like an 'o'. His hair was starting to grow back now, but in odd-shaped tufts, like a badly mown lawn. After every two steps he took an awkward kind of half step as if he'd suddenly changed his mind.

The black line above us was as thick as ever.

"Hwyl?" I said. "When you were on the boat, did you ever look up and see the stars?"

"Boat?" said Hwyl.

"Mm, there was one night when I was with Aunt Bea and the stars were really bright…"

Hwyl sniffed.

"I didn't come by boat," he said. "My mum gave me a lift."

"A lift?"

"Mum had to come with me, so we drove all the way from home…"

I couldn't believe my ears: she *drove*?

"But before that … didn't you come across on a big boat? And then get on the bus?"

"I've never been on a boat," he said. "I don't like water…"

I stopped and stared at his little round face, trying to work out what he meant.

"But our side … the big boat that took us across the bay…"

Hwyl looked at me his with big, sad eyes.

"Alex?" said Hwyl. "Can we stop now? I'm awful tired."

"With the big funnels?"

"I don't feel so good…"

"The ballroom and the dancing?"

"Alex, I need to stop now…"

"It'll be alright, Hwyl," I said. "We'll stop in a minute…"

The more I thought about things, the less they made sense. True, I couldn't remember Hwyl on board the ship – but then I couldn't remember Kieran and his trousers or any of the other kids either. Had they ever been on the boat? Had I? I tried to think but my head was full of *pottage*. If only I wasn't such a *nudnik*! "If you were any dumber they'd put a saddle on you and ride you into town" (Dad).

Confused, I let Hwyl go on a bit, carefully watching his funny little walk: one step, two step, half step, pause. From the back he looked like some kind of wind-up toy. What a goose, I thought, what a pup! Who knew "from whence he came…"

We were a long way from the school now, and a long way from the sea too. Eventually the fingers started to peter out again and we saw we were quite high up, on some kind of a ridge, or crag maybe. There were fields all around us and in some of them, big brown blobs.

"Look!" I said. "Cows!"

We walked the full length of the field, and then the next one, but all we saw was a low stonewall and plenty of pats.

"Maybe we could have a sit-down here," he whispered.

I wasn't so sure; the thick black line of the sky seemed very close and when I looked up I couldn't see a single star.

"Hwyl? Hwyl? Don't fall asleep…"

"I'm very tired…"

"Just a bit further…"

"I can't go any further…"

"But there's a house down there…"

"A house?"

"A house!"

"Really?"

"Really!"

It wasn't really a house though, not when you got close up. It only had half a roof and there wasn't any furniture in it or anything. Still: "who throws away a sock with only one hole?" (Grandy). I looked around both 'rooms' (though one was really only a yard) and found some rusted nails, a few bits of wood, a tin containing some kind of big blue tablets – I couldn't get the top off, though.

Still, "a hovel is a palace to a beggar" (Uncle Tomos) and Hwyl and I found a cosy nook by an inside wall, the two of us curled up together like two cats in a bag. It was surprisingly warm and snug in there and I dropped off almost immediately. How peaceful I felt! In my dream I was reading a letter from my mum. "Where are you, how can I find you?" she wrote. "Be happy and healthy, my dears. If only I could see you! But I travel further and further away…"

When I opened my eyes I could see big, bright, stars above me, round circles of light suspended in the sky. 'Is that you, my old friends?' I asked. 'So you've waited for me after all…' I wanted to take my shoes and socks off and follow them, but I felt too tired to move. How kind they were, how beautiful! I felt the same old pull, that familiar tugging at my heartstrings. Then, when I blinked again, the stars were gone and the sky was as black as tar. When I looked down there was blue all down my leg and the back of my puffer jacket seemed suspiciously wet.

"Hwyl?" I whispered. "Hwyl, did you see?"

I rolled myself over and flexed one leg. Blobs of turquoise snow drifted down through the hole in the roof and bits of glitter seemed stuck to the old stonewall. 'Like baby stars,' I thought, reaching out my hand. Then I noticed that Hwyl wasn't moving at all.

"Hwyl!" I whispered. "Hwyl!"

I tried to wake him but his eyes seemed gummed shut with some kind of goo, a grey slime not unlike that stuff they'd been feeding us, oh, these many weeks…

"Hwyl?"

Nothing. His eyes were sealed tight, his mouth a little straight line.

"Hwyl?" I said, prodding him a little with my foot. "Hwyl are you asleep?"

Confused, I stared at his little dark lids, his pale skin, the weird swirls on the top of his head. What strange patterns they formed! Rivers and seas and tufts. I gave him a little kick and watched him intently.

"Hwyl?" I said. "Hwyl are you dead?"

But then I saw his chest move and his little cheeks fill with air. 'No,' I thought, 'he's not dead yet!' Snow kept on falling. The light was very weird. 'When he wakes up,' I said to myself, 'I'll go climbing and Hwyl can make funny shapes in the snow.' I stared at the goo in the corner of his eyes and wondered whether to lick it. My head felt a bit heavy. The snow was blue and Hwyl was white. It was also very hot.

2

Because it was still dark, we weren't exactly sure how many meals we'd missed. Hwyl said it was three, but I said it was just one. Whatever it was, we both had the terrible hunger, and both felt a little dizzy too.

"Do you think we'll find something to eat soon?" he said.

"Mm," I said. I'd hidden the tin of blue pills in my puffer pocket, but I didn't say anything.

"Do you think they'll have crisps?"

"Sure."

Looking out over the barren landscape, it seemed terribly empty, as if made out of nothing. But of course it wasn't made of nothing – how could it be? – and instead it was made of this: snow, mud, a low stonewall, some kind of rough track.

We followed the track along the top of the ridge, looking out for any sign of life – a farm, a shop, even a bus stop. "Can you see the cable cars?" asked Hwyl and I pulled a funny face and spun my arms round like a windmill.

I was still thinking about what Hwyl had said earlier, I mean, about not coming here by boat and all. Something about his story "didn't sit right on my head" (Dad).

"Do you remember the captain?" I asked. "The one with the big hat shaped like a ship?"

"Is he in a cartoon?" asked Hwyl and I shook my head.

"I mean, on the boat. Or Seaman Able and his hairy hands?"

Hwyl rubbed his eyes sleepily. "I haven't been on a boat, Alex," he said.

"The scary birds?"

Hwyl shook his head.

"But if you didn't come on a boat then how did you get across to the other side?" I asked, feeling a little cross by now.

"What do you mean, 'other side'?" asked Hwyl, and I stopped and stared.

"What?"

Hwyl looked as confused as I did.

"What's the other side?" he said.

And that's when it finally clicked: if Hwyl hadn't come by boat ("ferry!") and didn't know anything about the bay – our bay, that is, the gap between the two sides – then it could mean only one thing: Hwyl was from *this* side instead…

Ach, what a trickster, what a fox! I'd let Hwyl play with me and eat with me and all the time "he'd saddled me like a mule" (Dad).

"I'm so hungry," he moaned. "Alex, are you hungry too?"

"Y-e-e-s," I said. My puffer jacket felt very tight.

"Do you think we'll find something to eat soon? My tummy is awful empty…"

What a shyster, what a "*schwine*" (Dr Kutchner)! But "I had the length of his nose" (Granny Mair)…

"Sure," I said. "You follow me…"

The ridge kept on climbing and the fields seemed a little stonier and drier, the snow more like powder up here, a mix of charcoal and dust.

"It's very high," said Hwyl. "Will we be at the cable cars soon?"

Looking back we could see a white road snaking its way through the gloom, as well as the headlights of the occasional lorry or van. So there were other people here after all! Their lights rolled across the empty ground, the road appearing and disappearing as they went. One moment things were there, the next moment they were gone.

"Here/gone/here/gone…"

"Alex?" said Hwyl, "do we have to keep climbing up? My feet are awful sore…"

I didn't look at him but instead picked my way between the stones and barbed wire; my jacket felt very warm and my pits were awful sweaty. Hwyl's head was poking out of his puffer like a newly hatched chick.

"Do you think Mummy will still be waiting?" asked Hwyl and I said, "I guess," and watched him with "both eyes open". 'So that's which side his bread is buttered!' I thought, darkly.

The track was a little more definite now, two straight tramlines across the silvery dust. I followed one and Hwyl walked along the other – one step, two step, half step, pause. The land kept on rising and when we reached the summit we could see just what it was we'd been walking toward all this time – a huge, wide cavity, big as the eye could see, the biggest crater I'd seen in my whole life.

"That's a big crater," said Hwyl, breathing in.

"Big as a house!" I said (though in fact, it was an awful lot bigger). It was so big it might have been one of the dimples – maybe even the nostril – that Bethan and I had seen from the boat. There were crusty ridges around the top, and then it fell away more quickly, with long furrows of snowy scree. It was a long way down.

"Alex?" said Hwyl. "Do you think other people come here?"

"I guess," I said.

"Do you think there might be somebody here now?"

"Maybe."

"Do you think they'll have food?"

"P'raps…"

We walked toward the edge of the crater, Hwyl's fuzzy little head leading the way. There were little craters and shadows on his noggin too.

"I'm very hungry Alex…"

The tufts and swirls on his head looked kind-of familiar, but where had I seen them before? They seemed to form patterns, shapes, seas…

"I could eat a horse…"

He was right on the edge of the cavity now, his little feet peeping out over the edge. The more I looked at him, the stranger he looked – like a cub that had just been shorn.

"Wooo, it's a long way down…" he whispered.

Craters, canals, bays … but where had I seen that little round head before?

"Do you think there's anybody at the bottom?"

Hwyl stared down into the crater, his thin, reedy voice drifting down into the darkness. "Hellooo…" he yelled. "Is there anybody there? Hello…"

He's trying to shout to the creature, I thought, he's calling to Mr Wolf! I watched Hwyl and my heart started to pound and there was a terrible squealing inside my ears.

"Alex? Can you shout as well? Alex?"

The whistling grew louder and I felt something hot and sour rising inside me. 'This is it!' I thought. 'It's coming, it's coming!'

"Alex?"

To be honest, I don't know what I was thinking. My head felt very hot.

"Alex, what is it?"

Before Hwyl could turn round I shoved him violently from behind, pushing him onto his front (how light he was, how thin!) and watching as he fell awkwardly, slipping down over the edge of the hole. When I raced forwards, I could see his little scribble sliding rapidly down the slope.

"Got you!" I yelled.

His puffer jacket twisted and dragged and I could see his arms flapping up and down.

"You're it, you're it, you're it…" I yelled.

His body slid down the hole but he didn't make a sound.

"Down, down, down the drain…"

When I looked down, Hwyl was lying in a funny star-shape just by a big round rock, snow (snow?) all over his face.

"Hwyl!" I yelled, "Hwyl!" Straight away I started to go after him. It was very slippery scrambling down the hole, but somehow I managed to keep my balance, arms out stretched, legs knee deep in the snow.

"Hwyl!"

He was lying in a very strange way, like a scrap of paper glued in the wrong place. All of him was there though, so why wasn't he moving? His face was very pale, his mouth sealed shut like an envelope.

"Hwyl?" I said.

I leant down next to him, checking him over for "vital signs" (Michael). Then I gave his body a little prod, and then tried rolling him about from side to side.

"Hwyl, wake up…"

Scared, I scraped the snow back from his face, and rubbed some of the bits off his mouth. Oh, why wouldn't he wake up? Not sure what to do, I tried twisting the top off the bottle of tablets I'd found in the out-house, little blue pills spilling out into the ground.

Hwyl's eyes were screwed shut, and he had a funny sort of mark on his head.

"Hwyl? Can you hear me?"

Not a flicker.

"Hwyl, are you there?"

Nothing. No, less than nothing, nothing take away nothing – the smallest thing in the world…

"It's okay Hwyl," I said, "this will make you better…"

I had the bottle of pills – well, slug-pellets – in my hands but suddenly my fingers started to shake.

"Hwyl, open up…"

Which was colder, Hwyl's cheek or the bottle of pills? I picked a handful of tablets out of the snow and tried pushing them in his face, but his mouth was squeezed into a tiny little dot and I couldn't get it open. When I finally got hold of his jaw he started to twist and grimace and I said, "No, Hwyl, eat these…" and he suddenly sat up and pushed me angrily aside.

"Alex, get off!" he yelled. "Leave me alone…"

With that, we both fell silent. Hwyl's face was covered in dust, just like the chalks we used at school. The mark on his head was a little bit black and a little bit red.

"You pushed me in," he said, baring his sharp little teeth. "You pushed me in and now I'm going back…"

I still didn't say anything – what should I say? My lips felt glued together.

"And when I get back I'm going to tell Miss Bedford and then I'm going to tell my mum and she's going to tell yours…"

I opened my mouth to say something but then thought better of it – "you can't put the leaves back on the trees" (Granny Mair). There was no point just standing there though, so we turned and started to clamber back up the bank, looking for foot-holds or rocks to hang on to. It took us quite some time. Both of us kept slipping but we didn't try to help each other. Neither of us said a word; we were both too tired, I guess.

When we got back to the top Hwyl glared at me with his deep, black eyes and said, "I'm going back to school now, Alex…"

School?

"But the teachers…" (I nearly said 'wolves' but thought better of it).

"My head is sore…"

It was hard to know what to say. Hwyl's voice was very shrill.

"But how will you get back?" I asked. "You don't even know the way…"

Hwyl looked at me like I was an idiot.

"The school is just over there, Alex," he said. "I'm stopping playing now…"

155

I looked back at the trees but couldn't work out what he meant. "But we've been walking for days and days…"

He scowled. "I don't want to play any more. I'm going back now…"

"Hwyl?"

"I'm not playing Alex…"

And with that he turned and walked away.

What could I say to him? That we were nearly at the cable car? That his mum was waiting? That I had some bright blue sweets?

"Hwyl, stop!" I yelled, but he didn't even turn to look at me. Instead I watched his little figure slipping and sliding in the snow: one step, two step, half step, pause. Well, if he thought that our school was just behind those trees, then 'more fool him'. "Good riddance to bad rubbish!" (Uncle Glyn). Who needed Hwyl with his weedy voice and his funny walk anyway? Those little legs of his – tch, they hardly reached the ground…

Oh, if only Bethan was still with me, I thought – she wouldn't have run off and left me. Why had I chosen Hwyl to come with me in the first place? Wade or Kieran or even boss-eyed Amelia would have been better. But I was all alone now – just like Mum crossing Russia. The snow, the cold, the empty sky. There was nothing now, nothing but this…

I watched Hwyl make his way over to the finger-trees – one step, two step, half step, pause – and then he disappeared too.

3

I don't know how far I walked after that, but it felt awful far, like "the long way round the world" (Granny Mair). Everywhere I looked the craters seemed strangely pitted and crumbly, half of them black and half of them blue. How strange it all seemed! A landscape of paper-maché and egg-boxes, a prospect of paste and paint and glue. It's true! You could almost read the newsprint, smell the resin, peel the white paste back from your fingers. Ah me, I thought; was I back in the school after all?

I could still see the wolf from time to time, crouched down behind a tree or hidden in the corner of my eye, its hair matted, ears pricked, a spoonful of saliva dribbling from his chops. But sometimes, when I looked just the right way, he looked more like a friendly animal from one of my story books, Mr Wolf dressed up in an apron and housecoat, some sort of bonnet on his head. Funny Mr Wolf! I could almost hear his breathing, smell his grown-up tobacco breath; sometimes he was the doctor and sometimes he was the captain and other times he was Mr Carver and his hairy ears, but all the time there was the same long tongue, a tangled mass of hair, those sharp black claws. 'I'm not in your tummy yet,' I thought, rubbing my own tummy thoughtfully...

The crater was far behind me now and the path started to drop away sharply. It was a real path now, a definite track, made by trucks and workmen and tarmac, and I followed it down until I came to a wide gate in the middle of a long metal fence, the bars terribly cold to the touch. When I climbed over I found myself by the side of a big, empty road, everything incredibly crisp and flat and even...

The road stretched as far as the eye could see, black as a marker pen and straight as a ruler. I wondered if I'd see any of the lorries bringing things to the new hotel, but they must have gone a different way – or maybe there were two roads, despite what Uncle Glyn had said. Poor me! Nothing came past, and then, a few minutes later, nobody came again. My hood was very tight. My feet were very sore. The snow felt kind of sticky and fell in funny lumps: mainly blues and greens but with the occasional yellow dab mixed in. The sky was crinkled, the snow roughly scumbled. Needless to say there weren't any trucks. Even the wolf seemed to have left me; when I turned round to look for him all I could see were his paw prints dotted across the page, a scattered line of tiny full stops. How lonely I felt! Like a mirror without a reflection, a cat without a shadow, a hat without a head... But then, "just as my poor heart seemed to falter" (Mum) the road took a sudden dip, revealing, 'as if from nowhere', a square house abandoned amongst the fields and the blobs and the night.

Such an apparition! The house was no more than a brick, a big, square box on its side. For a moment I thought that it was some kind of model abandoned in the snow, but as I made my way toward it, I realised that the house really *was* there, and just the right size too. As I crept closer and closer, the block seemed to grow more and more familiar, until finally I could see it for what it really was: Grandy's house, Grandy's house tied to a lamppost like a dog!

Ah me! It wasn't just that it *looked* like Grandy's house – it *was* Grandy's house, plucked from our little town and dropped here amongst the fields and the road and the darkness, "half way between nowhere and nothing" (Granny Dwyn).

But would my Bampa be in? As far as I knew, he was still cooped up in the bottom of the boat, "sick as a chicken in a pot" (Granny

Dwyn). Yet there was no doubt as to where I was: the gate, the old birdbath, the broken paving stone – this *was* Grandy's house, transported down to the last brick. Without knowing what I was doing, I ran to the front door and knocked three times. Grandy, Grandy/Old and thin/Open your door/And let me in! As soon as I said this I could hear locks being turned, bolts pulled back, and then there he was, blinking, yawning, scratching his head (hairier than I remembered it) and staring at me like something he'd fished out of a bin.

"What now?" he croaked, squinting at me with his cloudy eyes.

"What now?" I said. "It's me, Alex!"

"Alex?"

"That's right!"

"Alex?"

Who would have guessed his house would be so *big*? There were all sorts of doors and cupboards, and I thought to myself, 'How wide they are, and how dark!'

"Grandy, do you have any of those biscuits I like? The caramel ones?"

"Um…"

Grandy looked kind of confused, though whether this was because of his long trip, the lateness of the hour, or the blow to his head, I didn't know. *Was* it the middle of the night? Grandy was dressed in his pyjamas and dressing gown (blue, with a white star) and looked like he'd just come to.

"…though any biscuit will do…"

"Biscuit?"

"I'm starving!"

"Hm…"

"And I've come a very long way…"

Grandpa grunted and I skipped cheerfully into the 'sitting room', settling myself down in a big easy chair. But why was Bampa looking at me so strangely? True, I'd got blue all over his carpet and rug but still: who wouldn't take in a little boy all on his own on this dark and endless night?

Before I had time to look around properly, never mind play with any of his 'knick-knacks', Grandy returned, armed with a tray, a mug of coffee and a small plate of biscuits.

"There you are," he said. "Biscuits."

"Mm."

"That's what you wanted wasn't it?"

"Mm."

I took a sip from the mug and felt my eyes start to expand in my head.

"So…" he said. "Alex, yes?"

"Mruumph," I said, trying to fit as many biscuits in my mouth as possible. I felt a little uncomfortable with Grandy staring at me like that. What did he want me to say? Grandy had grown a lot of hair since the last time I'd seen him, and was a little shorter, too.

"Do you want the fire on?" he said, and I nodded though to be honest I was pretty hot to start with.

"Another cushion?"

"M'okay."

The mannie settled down into the chair opposite me and continued staring at me. I wanted to ask him about the boat and whether he had heard about the new hotel or Mum and Dad but I figured I'd hang on a bit 'cause my mouth was full of biscuit.

"These biscuits are nice," I managed finally.

The fella nodded and continued to stare. "Come a long way, lad?" he said at last. His voice was very low.

"From the other side," I said, cheerfully.

"The other side?"

"Mm. It was a long time on the boat. Did you get sick, Bampy? I mean, being in the hold and all?"

"Well…"

"We saw you, you know. Bethan and I. When you were with Auntie Glad. Is she here too? I was with Michael but he had to go to Big School and we got split up. Then I was with Hwyl, but he fell down a hole."

I paused and drank some more coffee.

"Grandy? Did someone bring your house over here? Do you think somebody will bring our house across too?"

He didn't answer but looked at me thoughtfully.

"You look awful wet son. Do you want your jacket off?"

"M'okay."

"Your shoes?"

"No, m'okay." I looked down at all my blue footprints but luckily the fella didn't seem to mind.

"So… is it a long way, then? This other side?"

"It took us *ages*," I said. "Luckily Michael had Dr Kutchner and I had Bethan and Mum and Dad had Auntie Bea and Uncle Glyn. Later on Michael had Mabel and I had Hwyl, but then Mum no longer had Dad and by the end we didn't even have Auntie Bea and Uncle Glyn any more."

"Mm," he said. His eyes were very red.

"They went up a cable car with Hwyl's mum. Mum went to look for Dad. Dad is building the new hotel. Do you know where it is? Is it near here?"

"A hotel?"

"Dad's in charge of the swimming pool. He's putting in the slides…"

Grandpa went quiet then, and if it hadn't been for the way his eyes were looking at me, I would have sworn that he'd fallen fast asleep.

"Grandy?"

He didn't answer but just kept on looking at me, a mess of white hair falling down over his eyes. Where his pyjamas met his dressing gown I could see a tuft of white hair poking out like a cat.

"Stay there, son," he said. "I'll fetch you a blanket so you can sleep…"

I was sweating terribly but I didn't say anything. The old man shuffled off toward the stairs and I got up and took a quick squizz at some of the photos propped up around the place. Oddly, Michael and I weren't in any of them – or Mum and Dad, or any of our three grannies for that matter. There was one kid who looked a bit like me, standing next to a plastic dinosaur with people I'd never seen before, but when I looked at it again, I turned out to be a little girl.

In fact when I thought about it, almost nothing about Grandy's 'sitting room' seemed right, not even the paper on the walls. I walked over to the far door and could hear hushed voices whispering on the other side. Was Grandy talking with Auntie Glad? I was jiggling about so much after my big cup of coffee it was hard to hear. Wee, wee, widdly wee! There weren't any biscuits left so I went to have a look in the kitchen instead, but even this seemed kind-of different to how I remembered it. I mean, I couldn't see Grandy's 'famous table' or his hat stand or even the brass horses I liked playing with. Confused, I wandered over to the window and looked out at the little garden, but it was really too dark to see. True, there were some trees and some kind of shed and a fence but everything looked awfully hazy and very badly painted. A little lost now, I turned back to look at the kitchen. Apart from the backdoor, there was another little door, possibly the door to the larder or pantry or something. Was this where Grandpa kept his biscuits? I took a couple of steps toward it but then I heard a loud whining start up from the other side.

"Hello," I said. "Hello, are you Grandy's dog?"

The whining turned to growling and then to a series of short, sharp barks. "Good boy. Clever boy," I said. "Do you want to play with a ball?"

The barking seemed to get louder and I started to back away.

"Do you want a pat?" I said. But then I had a thought: what if it wasn't a dog after all? Standing there in Bampa's kitchen, I didn't feel sure about anything. Where was I anyway? Grandy's kitchen had a big long dresser and smelt of gas; this one had a washing machine and a boiler and smelt of dog. In fact, come to think of it, Grandy's kitchen didn't look onto his garden at all…

Just then the thing in the larder suddenly banged against the door and I stumbled backwards and crashed into the washing-up. The dog (dog?) kept barking and jumping and I felt my bladder start to ache. Tch, if only I hadn't drunk that coffee! Tears came to my eyes, and further down too. The dog in the cupboard sounded like it was going berserk: what could it smell, little boys?

Then there was another bang and even more frantic scratching. I took two steps backwards and looked around for the door. That beast, those teeth, those jaws!

"Good doggy," I said. "Who's a good doggy?"

Silence.

"Shhh. Good boy. Stay…"

Nothing.

"Doggy?"

I felt something large and hairy on my back and that's when my bladder emptied *spectacularly*. Fuzz, claws, fur! I slipped on the lino but then made it out into the hall, something hot and sour breathing right in my ear.

"Son?"

I could feel its fetid breath, smell the fur, feel its claws pulling at me. Mr Wolf/Mr Wolf/All shaggy and hairy/Mr Wolf/Mr Wolf/All hungry and scary… The barking was "inconceivable" (Michael).

"Alex?"

The next thing I knew I was struggling with the door latch and stumbling out into the garden, "that dark and endless sea…"

"Alex, wait…"

"Like shit off a stick" (Cousin Cadoc) I took to my heels and ran toward the only cover I could see – a few spindly finger-trees ringed around a big black hole. Behind me the barking was *diabolical*, but

I didn't look back: "even the devil respects a clean pair of heels!" (Granny Mair). Just behind the trees was some kind of gully, a big wet drop, filled with all sorts of stuff – trolleys and bedsteads and black plastic bags. Shaking with fear and coffee, I stumbled down the bank, almost falling into the dark purpley liquid at the bottom.

If anything the barking and snapping sounded even more frantic, but I didn't look back. Instead I peered uneasily into the gloom, terrified of catching a flash of sharp teeth, a shock of white hair, the shadow of a paw. But no, there was nothing down there: nothing but me.

My head was very hot and my bottom half was purple. I lingered there for a moment, listening out for anything hairy or hungry. When I was sure that nothing had come down the bank after me, I started to splash my way along the gully, my special shoes sinking deep into the paste. It was very sticky and I was shaking terribly. My eyes felt as wide as a frog's.

After a few minutes I fumbled in my pocket and took out an imaginary walkie-talkie.

"Alex to Michael," I said. "Come in, Michael. This is Alex. Over."

No answer.

"Michael, can you hear me? This is Alex. Over."

The gully was very dark.

"Michael, do you copy? This is Alex. This is Alex. Over."

Then I waited.

"Michael?"

4

The gully led to a huge concrete pipe into which the purpley liquid seemed to disappear. I tried staring into its mouth but it was terrifyingly dark – and besides, a rusted metal grill blocked the way. Uncertain, I scrambled up one side and slid onto the top of the pipe; it was coated in a kind of thick slime but I didn't know where else to go – "where the monkey keeps his nuts?" (Cousin Huw).

One leg on either side of the pipe, I gingerly edged my way along its slippery length, eventually reaching some kind of concrete block at the far end. Beyond this the ditch seemed to come to an end, and the trees gave way to open ground. Climbing down from the funnel I could see a number of big tyre marks in the snow, the rutted ground leading to a flat, ugly-looking patch of open ground. The place looked like some kind of building site, with some bits taped off whilst the rest were split up by a series of low portakabins. The cabins were grey and the mud was blue, but the main thing, the thing you couldn't take your eyes off, was a great white wall, straight as a guillotine, cutting off the rest of the world from view.

What a sight! The wall stretched in both directions, without mark or opening or gate, higher than the highest house, wider than the widest field, an enormous, eye-watering straight line. Was this what Dad had been building? Maybe this was why he'd been gone for all that time, why so many people from the hotel had been needed, how they'd managed to fill that big long bus... But why would anybody build a wall smack in the middle of nowhere? And if it had been folk from our old snowy hotel, where were the workers now? I thought about hanging around for a bit, just to see if any of the brickies might turn up, but the place seemed kind of empty, truth be told: the huts were locked, the machines covered with plastic sheeting, the piles of building materials abandoned to the snow. No, there was nothing else to do but follow the long straight wall and look for some kind of gap. Where that gap might lead to, I tried not to think about; was the new hotel on the other side?

I tried to imagine what the hotel might look like, its breakfast bar and the pool, but for some reason my imagination seemed to fail me. Tch, maybe it was better this way – who knows? Maybe it's better not to be able to see over that line, to look straight out, "clear as glass" onto the other side. What was there to see anyway? "When you look into the void, the void sees also" (Uncle Tomos).

Fortunately the ground had been trampled down in front of the wall, so it was easy enough to follow it – the only thing was to figure out which way to go. First I walked left, tracing the wall as it cut through a little copse of trees, but then I changed my mind and went right, feeling my way along the line as it stretched across some kind of wasteland, stepping between the nettles and the bin bags, trying to keep my special shoes out of the mud.

Still, "if there are two ways to jump then you'll find two holes" (Dad), and after a while I turned back yet again, this time retracing my awkward little footsteps, back toward the trees. What else could I do? The wall was so long, it had to be the wall of something: but what? It certainly looked very strong. Whatever it was made of – brick, stone, concrete – it felt astonishingly smooth, like it was one long thing. I tried pressing my ear to it, but couldn't hear anything; then I looked around for a toehold but couldn't make out any indentations either. What a trick, what a swizz! From where I was standing, the wall seemed to go on forever, from here to eternity, from home to Timbuktu…

Every once in a while you had to push your way past a spindly thorn bush, and occasionally you could make out footprints or even wheelbarrow tracks where the workers had been, but otherwise there was nothing to see at all. There were no markings or signs of any kind: no graffiti, no stains, no nothing. It was without scratch or hole or abrasion, untouched in any way, clean as tomorrow's snow. Ah, if only I could have scribbled on it! But I didn't have a pen or a pencil or any kind of brush at all...

Not knowing what else to do, I trudged along beside it, all sorts of strange things going on inside my head. Mikey, big school, the hairy doctor and the wolves: everything felt oddly inconsequential now, as if it were some kind of fluey dream, or maybe a nursery rhyme from a book...

Poor me, poor Alex! Was it my imagination, or did the wall seem to bend slightly? But even if it did, even if it bent like a bow, I couldn't see how that could help me. I was alone, abandoned, lost on the Russian steppes...

It was only when I stopped feeling sorry for myself and started to look "with my eyes" (Mum) that I noticed something was different, something had changed, though what this was, I couldn't quite say...

I mean, the wall was still there, as white and un-climbable as ever – the snow blue, the mud wet. But then it came to me; tch, why hadn't I noticed before, how come I didn't see? The wall was no longer on my right, but somehow, on my left. How had it got there? How had it moved? I turned to look at it and it was as tall, as impenetrable, as imposingly blank as ever. Little mother, how had I missed it? When had it changed? What was once on one side was now on the other: such a thing! And with that I turned around and looked down over the hill, down over the bay, my breath forming a little speech bubble in the gloom...

The Bay of Doubles

1

It was both our town and not our town. The hills were the wrong shape, the sea-wall bent, Knob Rock on the wrong side of town. It was only when I got a little closer that I realised what the problem was: the whole place – the houses, the shops, the streetlights, the "entire kit and caboodle" (Dad) – was only half-built. No, really! There were signs of construction everywhere: piles of sand, stacks of timber, cement-mixers, bricks. Some bits were sealed off by high metal-fences whilst others had been left wide open, exposed to the elephants ("elements!" – Michael). Sharp poles, deep holes, barbed wire, and all the time I was able to wander wherever I liked, "free as Adam in his youth" (Uncle Tomos). Only one thing worried me: why was everything so badly made? Doorways put in skew-whiff, windows that wouldn't close, outer walls that didn't quite meet. Ach, what a dump! It looked like it had been made by builders who'd heard of our little town, but never actually seen it. The whole thing seemed knocked up in haste, unfinished, abandoned. Ho, what a sad fate for our poor little town! To be turned into a third-rate copy of itself, a kind of double or a shadow, and a shadow's shadow at that...

There were pipes sticking out of the walls and cables hanging down from the ceiling, steps built in the middle of the street and alleyways that went nowhere. Tch, who could live in a place like this? One house had had its front door fitted half way up a wall; another was built on such a slant you could have rolled a penny from one side to the other. "Either my eyes are wrong or your working-out!" (Grandy). Confused, I clambered up onto a pile of rough pallets and peered in between the strips of grey tarpaulin. One wall of the room sloped up, another tipped down, and the door was caught out in the middle. "Found you, found you!" I yelled.

My head sore, I found myself a long metal pipe and went around hitting things: pallets, portakabins, windows. Afterwards I went over to one of the many piles of bricks and played 'shot-put' and 'bomb' but it was still pretty dull. No lights clicked on, no grown-up came. I tried throwing stones up at the roof tiles but they all slid back down, some of them narrowly missing my head. Ah, if only Hwyl had been here! Then we might have played a proper game, with running and pushing and everything. But instead I just drifted amongst the unfinished blocks, scuffing my shoes on the wooden pallets, jumping from the big concrete blocks into the blueish snow. "Grrr," I said, a little half-heartedly.

If only it wasn't all so sloppy! Lines didn't meet, blocks weren't coloured in, things were either too big or too small. Even if you had one foot on the pavement, the other ended up in the gutter. Tch, such a mess, such a botch-job! Surely my dad hadn't had a say in this – he had "the eyes of a sharpshooter" and "the hands of a surgeon" (Dad). Ah, was the new hotel going to be just like this? To stay another week amongst the craters and the snow "didn't sound like a bargain to me" (Aunt Bea). For all I knew this building site went on forever, "cock-eyed as a bulldog's squint" (Uncle Glyn). Of its builders, I didn't want to know; when I looked across at the sagging pasteboard walls I thought, 'No, not here,' and when I looked up at the bulging wallpaper roofs I thought 'No, not here either.' But what was I to do? Everybody has to be somewhere, even little boys... And so I buzzed from door to door, "like a bumblebee in the winter" (Granny Mair), my shoes more and more clogged with blue...

Sometimes the town felt like an enormous playground, but other times it felt like wandering through the workings of a giant workshop, the whole place smelling of timber and glue and paint. The worst houses were those made of paper-maché and cardboard, but even the brick ones looked hastily cobbled together, as if haphazardly assembled in the dark (and of course it *was* dark, a cave without beginning or end...) What was a boy to do? I wandered from plot to plot, avoiding the ditches and the sink-holes, my shoes ruined "beyond hope of resurrection" (Mum). I mean, there wasn't even a proper road – just big wide tracks made by diggers or concrete mixers or something, great furrows churned up in the mud and the sand. You could either walk along the top of the track or down in the hole, it didn't really matter. What did matter? "The colour of your tongue, the size of your hat, the hole in your pocket" (Uncle Tomos). And yet...

I stared all around me, mouth open, tongue out. Who would choose to live in such a place? Crooked roofs, leaning walls, lampposts which seemed to bend down to the ground; I felt dizzy just looking at them. All around me were odd-shaped shadows, sudden drops, mismatched steps: no wonder my eyes rolled "like Uncle Glyn on payday" (Dad). But despite all the weird blocks and strange angles, I couldn't help but feel that something here was known to me – the corner where the newsagent's once stood, a sandpit where the swings used to be, the spiky railings of our library, the sharpest railings in the world…Yes, the more I walked on, the more it looked like our own little town, if not its twin, then at least a distant relation. There was the fire station, the TV mast (a little bow-legged, but still…), the humpy-backed bridge: all of them in the right place, though not necessarily the right shape, I'll grant you that…

I could even walk in a more or less straight line now. The pavement (pavement!) looked flat, the road flush to it, the lines pointed, more or less, in the right direction. Such a thing! Even the buildings seemed a little better – walls painted, edges finished off, glass fitted. True, the paint hadn't completely dried in places and some of the colours seemed to have gone over the lines, but at least I knew where I was now. "Home again/that dear old hearth and stove…" Yes, it was all looking kind-of familiar – the empty playing fields, the deserted changing huts, Cemetery Road, the way bending right (to Hell) or left (to the sea). And through the blue snow, blue fog, though the fog smelt of glue not the sea…

"Fog," I said. "Fog, fog, fog."

The fog said nothing.

2

There was no traffic, no people. I didn't see a single cat or a solitary bird (of course, it *was* still night – but then it had been night for as long as I could remember). Either our little town was deserted or else everyone was tucked up in bed, "dreaming tomorrow's dreams" (Mum). And how blue it all was! Blue shops, blue houses, blue snow: even the traffic lights were blue. Where was all this light coming from anyway? The black line of the sky was so thick the stars didn't dare peek through.

I zigzagged across the roads and roundabouts, leaving little birdlike specks in the snow: one step, two step, half step – jump! How dizzy I felt! The air had a sweet, chemically smell that made my head spin and my feet trip. In places the fog looked as thin as tissue paper, in others as thick as porridge. Melted snow collected in oily-looking puddles. The shadows were as solid as barricades.

And yet, for all that, the walls, the gardens, the shop-fronts – they all seemed known to me, as close as the nose on my face. It's true! The chemists', the hairdressers', the half-built tower with the bars on its window – all of them were there, like ticks on a register. But how could this be? I mean, if they'd carried our little town – parks, roads, bridges and all – if they'd carried it clear across the ocean (sea!), loading it into boxes, then onto boats and over planks, before finally lugging the whole lot through the snow to here – well, if they (they?) had done this, then what had happened to all the people left behind? Old Mrs Griffith and the McAuleys who ran the newsagent's and my three grannies and everybody else? And yet if they had built this funny little town for us – this cartoon, this caricature, this funny little squiggle – then where were all the people from the boat? Dr Kutchner, Bethan, the Mirozeks, Dr Morgan… No, I couldn't work it out. The right buildings were in the wrong place. The trees on Bryn-y-dwn were the wrong size. The stream by the substation ran downhill, not uphill. Was this home or no? The more I thought about it the less certain I became. There were too many shadows. The houses had funny faces. Finger-trees were hiding between the alleys and the shop-fronts. "Shoo," I hissed as I ran past the eye-holes. "No peeking at little boys…"

But had our house really been moved here, plonked down like a coffin in a plot? It seemed very hard to believe. I mean, what if our house was missing and there was just a great black hole? Or what if it was there, but full of great hairy wolves, sharpening their claws and licking out the pots? All at once my skin crawled and I felt beads of sweat trickling down my back. If only my head wasn't so sore, my hood so tight! Yet for all that my feet kept carrying me there, my feet, my legs, my special shoes. Mm, it's true: "the blackbird must find its nest" (Granny Mair). And then there it was, right in front of me: our castle, our semi, "the dear old family spread"…

What a sight to bring in the light! Our wall, our drive, our tree, even my broken plastic tank in the garden – all exactly as we'd left them, just like the day (day?) we'd packed our bags ("two suitcases only") and gone down the hill, "down to the sea in ships…" (Dad).

The same flowerbed, same broken garage door, same prickly hedge: ah, those sharp, spiky leaves, those sweet, poisonous berries! Yes, it was all still here and it hadn't changed a bit. Or had it? The top storey didn't seem to sit quite square on the lower, the hedge looked like it had been dug up and transplanted, the guttering hanging loose from the side. Still, "what careth the heart for such things?" (Mum). It was still home, or at least the nearest thing to it. "If not here, then where?"

In a feverish daze I trotted along the garden path and toward the front door. The grass was a brilliant shade of turquoise. The drive was the colour of Aunt Bea's dress. The door felt kind of wet and tacky, as if the paint hadn't quite had time to dry. Still, when I pushed against it, it opened like a dream.

Inside, everything had been set up just right – though of course *our* carpet was a kind of sandy brown rather than this deep blue. The kitchen was much the same though – blue washing machine, blue table, blue curtains, as if the same thick brush had been used for all. The lounge was kind-of blue too, but the TV was switched off, and the table strangely empty. The cushions were all bunched up at one end of the settee but otherwise the place looked untouched. No books scattered around, no pictures, no footprints on the rug – it could have been a room in a hotel or a picture in a book. I mean, where was everybody? I'd pictured Michael and his schoolbooks, Mum and her Russians, Dad and Uncle Glyn talking engines… But no, here – here was nothing. Nothing take away nothing. Maybe even less than that…

Breathing hard, I turned away from our front room (where nobody ever went anyway) and climbed the crooked, crooked stairs. The door to Michael's room lay open and I could see his bed, his stacks of modelling magazines, the chess set *not to be touched*. There were school textbooks laid out on his desk, a calculator, paper, pens, a protractor: my brother, the scholar! The door to Mum and Dad's room was closed and though I rested my ear against it, I didn't open it – who knows why? Nor did I go to the bathroom, although, now I come to think of it, I hadn't 'been' for a very long time. No, I simply followed the landing to my own little room, my nest, my nook, my cosy den… After all, this was it, the final test: was I home or no?

Inside, the curtains were drawn and my toys were scattered everywhere – diggers, concrete mixers, space ships. A pack of felt-tips lay open on my plastic table, next to a drawing of a boat. The sky was a big black line and it seemed to be snowing blue. Was that a picture of a lion or a bear above my bed? Its expression was very fierce and its mouth was very large. My posters were all there, but looked like they'd been re-arranged somehow, the top ones on the bottom and the bottom ones on the top. Other things, though, were 'spot-on'. My wardrobe was full of comics. Various football stickers were stuck to my mirror. On the stool nearest to my bed sat floppy dog, who I hadn't seen for the longest time. Wordlessly I picked him up and inspected his butt. Yes, it was really him: same hanging-off ear, loose label, long tail. The only thing different was a logo reading 'Property of White Star Shipping Company' stamped on one paw. 'Yes, everything is owned by someone,' I thought. There was a funny stain on one wall. My room smelt of timber and glue. I put floppy dog back on the chair and rested my head on the bed.

At first I couldn't work out why I didn't feel happy. All my toys were okay. Our house was still in the right place. Nobody had taken anything or smashed things up. And yet for all that it didn't feel like anything was *mine* – more like looking at a room in a museum, or a kind of kit or model.

But the main thing I felt was tired. Oh, if only I could sleep! I fumbled with the zipper on my puffer jacket, but still couldn't get it to open. Nor could I work out what to do with my shoes. What had they said about them back at the hotel? "A shiny shoe is a point for you" – but I might have been mixing things up. I felt awful woozy. My pits were wet but my lips were dry. What a state I was in! I couldn't work out if I was getting dressed or taking my clothes off, whether it was night or day. Instead, like the red duck in the story, I got into bed and climbed under the covers "just as I was".

In an instance the sheets were stained blue, but what could I do? The bed was kind-of blue already – everything was. I thought about Mum and Dad, and then I thought about Michael and Mabel, and then about Aunt Bea and Uncle Glyn, and after a while the room turned from blue to black and I didn't think about anything at all.

3

Did I dream? I don't think so. I was too tired to dream. When I woke up a great hairy face was staring down at me, a long red tongue flicking between his whiskers.

"So, how are you feeling my lad? Any stronger?"

"Mm," I said, watching the big, long tongue dart from side to side.

"That's a good lad. You're a big strong boy now aren't you?"

"Yes sir."

"Clever boy! Now let me just look in your eyes…"

He shone some kind of light in my eyes and for a moment I couldn't see a thing.

"Hm," he said. "Like two hard boiled eggs! And poke out your tongue…"

I did it.

"Ah! Pink as a thick slice of ham! Now let me look in your ears… Mm, mm, very good – two little cauliflowers, ready for the plate! Well, you're a fine little dish, make no mistake…"

"Yes sir."

"Now I need to take a little look at your chest. That's it, hold still…"

He undid the top button of my pyjamas (I don't know what had happened to my puffer) and pressed two fingers against my skin.

"Splendid! You'll out-live us all. And breathe in…"

His fingers were ten hairy caterpillars; his nails were very black.

"And out…"

Ach, how close his face was! I could feel the bristles on my chin, stare up his nose, smell the sandwich (sandwich?) he'd had for lunch. But I didn't want to venture too far into that mouth. No sir! If you climbed in there you'd never get out alive…

"And in again… and out … that's it lad, full of the breath of life…"

He smiled at me and his mouth was enormously wide, a huge black gap in his beard.

"Doctor Bumble? I ate all my grey and made sure I kept my shoes on…"

"Shhh! You're a clever boy, but you haven't been very well. That's why we had to bring you here. Do you remember? You're a big boy, I'm sure you remember…"

"Yes sir…"

"There's a fine lad."

Hair hung down from his nostrils like creepers, mixing with the thick black undergrowth on his chin. His lips were wet and his teeth very sharp.

"Would you like a drink Alex?"

"Yes please."

"There you are, drink this, there's a good lad. Oh, and pop this pill in too…"

I drunk the water and watched him flick through a thick pile of papers; his nails looked surprisingly dirty for a doctor.

"Sir? Is it still night?"

He smiled. His mouth was like a huge gash in the middle of his face, a kind of crevasse.

"Yes, it's still night, Alex."

"For just a little longer?"

"Just a little longer."

I thought about this and watched him attach the file to the end of my bed.

"Sir, why is the snow here so sticky? Well, sometimes it's powdery, it depends…"

The doctor was fiddling around with some kind of pager and didn't say anything.

"Michael says that it's not snow at all, but I don't know. Is it because of the snow that we have to wear our special shoes? Or is it to stop us from bumping our heads on the sky?"

He sniffed the air and placed one shaggy paw on my forehead.

"Is it so we don't float up into space?"

"Shhh, rest now Alex. Don't worry your head about such things. You have to concentrate on getting better, do you understand?"

"Yes sir."

"There's a good lad. Now you try and get some rest, sweet prince. That's it. Lay back down. You're a strong boy and no mistake."

"Thank you sir."

"That's my lad, sleep. Sleep. And we'll talk again in the morning..."

"Morning?"

"Shhh. Sleep, sleep... There's a good little boy... sleep."

So I did.

When I saw the shadow I hoped it might be Mum or Dad or even Aunt Bea or Uncle Glyn, but instead it was Mr Carver, smelling of cigarettes and sitting on the edge of my bed with a bowl of steaming 'pottage'.

"Alex? Time to eat. That's it, prop yourself up. You have to eat it all up if you want to be big and strong..."

Yes, it was him: beady eyes, flat nose, hairy ears. I glanced at his ears suspiciously: who knew what horrors lurked within?

"Come on Alex, push yourself up. Do you want me to feed you? Well, open your mouth. There we go..."

I didn't like Mr Carver being in my bedroom. It was still dark. The light from behind the curtains was blue.

"That's right, open wide..."

What could I do? I was tired. I was hungry. The spoon was in front of my face.

"That's it. And another... good boy."

He followed my spoon like a vulture follows a starving man. His head was bald but his ears were full of wool. Truth be told, his chin could do with something of a shave, too.

"Are you feeling better, boy?"

"Mm," I said, mouth open.

"Much stronger?"

"Mm," I said, mouth closed.

"Not so achy?"

"Mm," I said, sucking on the spoon.

"Just so, just so." He paused and seemed to look at something I could not see.

"It's good to see you looking so well, boy."

He moved a little closer.

"So well and so plump."

His mouth was very close to me now.

"There's just one thing lad," he said. "One tiny thing. Tell me Alex: how did you and your little friend sneak out?"

My mouth opened but no spoon went in.

"It's all right my lad, you can tell me, you won't get into trouble now. I just need to know how you got out."

I opened and closed my mouth like a fish. It seemed vitally important that I say the right thing now but I couldn't work out what that might be.

"Eh, my bonny lad?"

He stared at me with a fearful intensity. His face was awful close.

"That night you ran away, d'you remember? What did you do at the big fence, Alex? How did you get over?"

He moved the spoon toward my face and my mouth opened up without my knowing it.

"Don't worry Alex, nothing will happen to you. We just need to know. How did you manage to get out, lad? Was there somebody helping you? What happened to your little friend?"

It was very odd seeing Mr Carver sitting in my bedroom, amongst my toys and my comics, right next to floppy dog. Either he was the wrong person in the right place or else it was the other way round – it was very hard to tell.

"Alex? Alex, are you listening? Hwyl is very sick. We need to find him. Is he hiding someplace? Alex, look at me now..."

I didn't want any more goo. The spoon was dripping grey. Mr Carver's ears frightened me.

"Sir, I think I need to go back to sleep now..."

Suddenly all the muscles in his face seemed to twitch.

"Alex, we need to know what happened. Everybody was very worried about you – you and Hwyl. We need to know what happened to you after you left..."

I looked down at the remains of grey in my bowl. There were funny swirls and shapes streaked along the bottom and sides. I didn't feel so hungry now.

"Alex, you're not in trouble. Nobody will tell you off. But we have to find Hwyl before he gets too sick. Do you understand Alex? You're a clever boy – you understand what I'm saying..."

"Sir? I need to put my head back down on the pillow..."

"Alex..."

"I'm very tired sir..."

His voice was very quiet and level but his eyes were awful cruel – the same eyes as the gulls which had followed the ship.

"Did you leave him Alex? What happened to him? Why isn't he with you?

"I'm sorry sir, but I'm asleep..."

I closed my eyes and sank back down. Better bed than dead! Mr Carver was making funny little rasping noises and I imagined him squeezing floppy dog between long black claws.

"Alex?"

I felt his breath in my face and closed my eyes, "tight as Uncle Glyn's wallet" (Dad). Something was moving just above my head but I tried to ignore it. It was as if Mr Carver were circling high above me, swooping round and round my head. My hands were sweaty and my skin felt kind-of hot. But I didn't want to talk to Mr Carver or gaze into those horrible hairy ears. "If the lion's cage is empty, why invite him in?" (Grandy). No, better to shut my eyes and hope that he might disappear too.

"Alex…"

The swooping sound got louder. I could smell cigarettes, sandwiches, coffee, but I still didn't open my eyes.

"Alex?"

Eventually I heard the clatter of cutlery and the sound of my tray being carried away – maybe by Mr Carver, maybe by somebody else. I still didn't want to move. The pillow smelt very chemically. My face itched. Somehow it didn't feel like my bed at all; there were funny lumps and bulges and my feet seemed caught in some kind of under-sheet. And yet for all that I could feel myself drifting away into real sleep. Ah me, I thought – how easy it is for pretending to become the real thing! My limbs grew heavier, my body sank into the bed, and the bed sank into the ground. What a funny feeling! The sheets were like big waves on top of me, the pillow a great stone. The waves, the sea, the weeds: who would have thought that the sea would be blue all the way down? And the water – so clear, so blue, so strange! How would I feel when I got there? Washed, unmuddied? "There's nothing so clean as a fish" (Granny Mair). But why was the bottom so far?

When I came to, it was still night. The light from behind the curtains was an even deeper shade of blue. My covers had slipped a bit but my bed was still there – wherever 'there' might be.

I heard the door opening and quickly scrunched my face into the pillow, pulling my arms and legs up into a little ball. But this time the voice was kinder, gentler, a woman's.

"Alex?"

I squirmed in my bed but wouldn't look up. My face was very hot where it had been pressed into the pillow and I'd dribbled a bit too.

"Alex? Alex, it's time to go…"

When I turned over it was Miss Bedford brushing back my hair from my eyes, just as Mum might have done. Ah, sweet Miss Bedford! I'd almost forgotten her and there she was, standing in my bedroom, like she'd been pasted in onto the wrong page.

"Alex, your parents are waiting for you. Come on, Alex, you have to get up…"

Enormous hands seemed to pull back the covers and lift me out of bed. A yellow puffer jacket was placed over my pyjamas, special shoes squeezed onto my feet. Oh, Miss Bedford, what big hands you have! As big as my whole body, as big as the room…

"Your mum and dad are just down the corridor – Michael too. Come on, that's it – both feet on the ground. There's a brave lion…"

Her voice was very kind and very gentle, but I couldn't tell whether it was Miss Bedford or not. Still – "how sweet the pipe that calls the lost sheep home" (Auntie Glad). I rolled over to one side and felt the hands start to lift me up.

"They've been worried about you Alex – you haven't been very well. But it's okay; you can go and see them now. There's a good lad – off you go…"

Little Miss Bedford/so meek and so mild/ kind to her cats/and good to her child. How sweet she was! The only one of my teachers who'd ever shown me any tenderness, any love… But then the door was open and I was out in the corridor, back in my yellow puffer and special shoes, zipper zipped, laces tied.

"That's it Alex, they're just here…"

"Here?"

"Right in front of you Alex. You just have to open your eyes..."

I heard the words, but somehow they didn't seem to make sense. I mean it didn't look like our landing at all – more like one of the corridors from the hotel, kind-of functional and sterile looking. It's true! The walls were white and the carpet grey. There were notice boards and glass booths and even a telephone kiosk near the desk.

"Sir?" I said, looking back. "Are you sure my mum and dad are there? They've gone on to the next hotel, not this one."

But Miss Bedford (Miss Bedford?) merely smiled, circling my little body with her huge white hands.

"Shhh, you're in the right place now, Alex. Do you understand? They're waiting for you now. There isn't far to go." Her hands were incredibly soft but held me tight. "Can you see, Alex? There, just past the trolley and the lifts..."

I scrunched up my eyes but couldn't really see. All I could make out were shapes, blurs, drips...

"Yes sir, I see."

"Good lad, clever boy."

Was it Miss Bedford? All I could feel were those enormous white hands.

"Be good for your mum and dad. Take care Alex, goodbye..."

Oh Miss Bedford, so kind and so dear! I felt her hands on my shoulder but when I turned around, there she was – gone.

"Miss Bedford?"

Goodbye Miss Bedford! Goodbye Dr Bristle! Goodbye floppy dog!

And then I walked down the corridor and I was gone too.

4

The fog felt very heavy and very firm. It crept inside my puffer jacket and inside my hood, neither hot nor cold, wet nor dry. Was it fog? I didn't know – "does a spoon know the taste of soup?" (Grandy). Nor could I see my mum and dad: just shapes, smears, strange streaky lines. The funnel seemed to narrow, and I felt an incredible sense of pressure, like putting on a very tight jumper, or sliding down some kind of tube. The walls were very close now. The fog (fog?) was pressed against me like a mould. It was awful hard to breathe.

And then before I knew it, the fog cleared, just a bit. I wasn't here, but there, not this side, but the other. Yes, somehow I'd wandered far away from home, lost in a childish daze...

Poor me, how had I got here? One moment I'd been curled up in bed, the next I was out in the cold, wearing "six inch shoes in seven inches of shit" (Cousin Evan). The corridor (corridor?) seemed to go on forever, though I wasn't sure whether it was my hallway, a tunnel, or the street. The fog was so *deep*. 'Mummy and Daddy,' I thought. 'Where are you? What is this place?' Blobs, drips, spatters; yes, this time I really was all alone, "lonely as the last hair on your head" (Uncle Glyn). 'This isn't my hall,' I thought, arms outstretched, 'this isn't my house.' The fog wasn't just outside – it was inside too, up my nose, in my ears, gumming up my eyes. "Foul, foul, vapour!" (Uncle Tomos). All I could do was to push my way through it, blindly pushing on, arms outstretched, mouth tight shut. Fog, fog, fog! And then the fog pulled back and I was back in the town again, or rather, our town's evil twin, surrounded by fog and snow and scaffolding…

But how had I got from there (there?) to here (here?), from our house to this place – whatever this place might be?

It's hard to say. The houses were empty. The trees were sticks. I made my way along one of the little lanes that dropped down to the sea-wall, but even this lane, familiar as the inside of my fist, didn't somehow turn the way it should, twisting the wrong way, going up when it should have been going down, arching left instead of right. I know, I know: such a place! Such mystery!

The fog was made of cotton wool, the buildings of balsa and glue. 'What a con,' I thought, 'what a swizz…' I wandered over to one of the blue cottages but couldn't tell if the door was real or just painted on. Should I knock? Should I push? But what was the point? "You don't walk into a bear trap wearing your new fur coat" (Grandy). And so I went on, into the night, into the snow, half a pound of nothing, a bumblebee in wintertime…

If only I could retrace my steps, I thought, follow my footprints, plant my feet in familiar earth. Aye, there's the rub; how to get back to our side, our town, our street. I mean, what was between my ears – oatmeal? If I ever wanted to see my family – Grandy and Auntie Glad and my three grannies and of course beautiful Aunt Bea and naughty Uncle Glyn – if I ever wanted to see them again, then I had to go back across the water, ford the channel, cross that bay with neither paddle nor tiller nor boat…

Just think: on the other side of the bay was my real house, real school, real town. And maybe Mum and Dad and Michael were already there and waiting for me – not in a blue house on a blue street but back on the dear old earth. Yes, that must have been it! They were there already, back amongst the ordinary, at home amongst the known…

With "joy in my heart and a song on my lips" (Aunt Bea), I pushed my way through the fog and followed the curve of the road, skirting the taxi rank, the toilet block, the long back wall of the supermarket. And beyond that? Just one more road and then the wall, the beach, the beautiful briny sea! Mm, I could see it already – a solid block of blue, a straight black line, the empty page beyond…

Feeling a sudden surge of energy, I sprinted toward the wall and gazed out at the vast and limitless horizon – that divine line, that eternal strip, the bar between this world and the next. Yes, there it was – the divider, the limit, the threshold – long as a measuring tape and straight as a ruler. But how to cross it? The sea came in and the sea went out: all I had to do was to lie there and wait for the waves to carry me, sweep me clean across the bay. How do boats travel after all? Pushed from one side to the other by the tide, as any fool can plainly see ("I can plainly see that" – Uncle Glyn). Ho, what was I worrying my little head about? The water would hold me, the waves would push me, the stars would light my way… Ach, how far was the horizon anyway? No more than the tip of your finger or the end of your nose. Yes, it was only a short stretch to the edge, to that great dropping off point, after which, like the very top of a waterfall, it would be downhill all the way to the end… It's true! The brim, the brink, the tip. And after that? Why, our house, our garden, the green, green hills of home…

A little braver now, I started to look for some way down, some way of scrambling down from the wall to the very foot of the bay. The wall was so high, so black, so smooth – but after a few minutes of patient searching, I came upon a series of steep wooden steps, leading down to the beach below. Okay, the glue wasn't quite dry and the steps seemed to wobble, but still, down and down I went, the steps as crooked as Cousin Nona's teeth…

At the bottom, the beach was little more than a pile of builder's gravel, the stones all loose and slippery, spattered in places with paste and glue. There was a wheelbarrow and some kind of mixer to one side, and alongside that a pile of pallets, abandoned in a tall, dangerous-looking heap. Fortunately one pallet had fallen free, and as soon as I saw it, the wood kind-of rotten looking and one beam already broke, I knew I'd found my boat. True, there wasn't much room, even for a tiny, tiny boy, but if one foot should droop in the water, did it really matter? What did I care after all? When I got to the other side I'd never have to wear my special shoes again…

Even so, the gravel was hard and the pallet heavy. If you got a splinter in your hand then the wood could go straight to your heart – "death considers not the fairest forehead" (Granny Dwyn). Still, after much huffing and puffing, I managed to get the crate loose and drag it a few steps across the beach. It seemed a very long way. I couldn't hear the sea, but I knew it was out there. The fog was still very thick – like the gunk in Hwyl's eyes. The beach smelt of glue and paste. Sections of gravel were marked off with little sticks and wire, but I pulled the pallet across anyway. What was this – a beach or a building site? From where I was standing it was awful hard to tell. And yet for all that, I hauled the pallet across the shale and stone, my little arms seeming to come loose in their sockets…

I mean, who had made this thing – this ringer, this copy, this double – and why had they put it here, just across the channel? But even I had to admit that whoever had made the sea had done a really good job. The blue sheets of plastic were surprisingly convincing, and the waves seemed to ripple and move with the tide. Such realism! Such detail! Tentatively, I tested the waters with my foot and it neither tore nor twisted nor came apart. Instead I was able to balance my little boat on the surface, clambering onto the pallet without so much as a wet sock. Yes, there I was, captain of my ship, king of the ocean waves! And before I knew it – before I knew anything – my little pallet was bobbing erratically on top of the waves, my head perched above it like a gull.

The waves splashed (how life-like they were!), the boat swayed, but my little vessel, ah, she stayed "ship-shape and Bristol-fashion" (Dad), bobbing about like an apple in a barrel. How sturdy she was – how safe! For now the sea really was carrying me – carrying me further and further out, away from the wall, away from the beach, away from that makeshift little town. It's true! With every passing minute the shore seemed a little less clear, its outline a little more blurry. And that's when the fog descended, that same blue fog, like smoke from a thousand fires... 'Oh fog, fog, do your worst,' I thought, 'the sea will carry me now...'

Mm, the fog rolled in and the shore vanished, but I was still there, even if I was only a "gnat's length" above the water-line. Besides, the channel wasn't that wide, little more than a gap really, the closest point between here and there...

It was just like that time on the ice: to the side of me darkness, ahead blobs, marks, little streaks of ink. I turned round but the fog had already rubbed out the outline of the crooked little town. I could just about make out the twisted spire of a steeple, maybe even the shadow of Knob Rock, but that was about it. My tub bobbed up and my tub bobbed down: what else should it do? Instead I concentrated on that great fake sea, the long sheets of blue and green, the crisp rustle of the waves. What a job they'd done on it: such work, such finishing! To either side of me the fog billowed and blew, but above me the darkness seemed to thin slightly, and I could see tiny glimmers of fire, little specks of white. Was it my old friends, the stars? Excited, I lay on my back and gazed up at them. Yes, the clouds were moving, and with them the darkness. Here and there tiny pinpricks of light could be made out, tiny droplets of cream. 'Where have you been?' I thought. 'Why did you abandon me?' And then there were hundreds of them, a whole ocean of light, more real and more certain than the very waters beneath me... The stars spiralled and the heavens swam. My friends, my friends! The stars splashed across the sky in great streaks of white, leaving tiny blobs of light in their wake, miniscule drops of celestial milk. It was just like that night with Aunt Bea, so strange and so fair. Ah, if only I could join them! If only they could lift me up, carry me off, take me away from this makeshift world once and for all…

The more I stared, the closer and brighter the stars seemed to come. Were they up in the sky or inside my head? I tried blinking, but the stars were still there, only an arm's length away now, no more than the fingers on your hand.

It's true! The stars spun and the heavens turned, and I felt everything inside me start to float upwards, my trainers, my jacket, even the hairs on my head. Was this it? Was I finally going to float free? But then I glanced back to earth and saw the sodden wood, the broken cross-beam, the inky water below. One of my trainers was already wet; my bottom felt cold and vulnerable.

"Sir?" I said.

You might think that the stars would be reflected in the black sea, but they weren't. Looking down was like staring into a big pool of nothing. No, the weight of the world is no small thing, I thought. Up above the stars turned and down below the darkness gaped. But what if they should change places? My arms twitched, my legs too, and I felt that pull, that same pull Mum must have felt before she took off across Russia, or Aunt Bea and Uncle Glyn getting on the cable car or even Dad looking back at us from the bus…

"Sir?"

My feet now both felt wet, the cold spreading steadily up my legs. Ach, there was no doubt about it: the pallet was definitely sinking. But what could I do? The water was very cold – almost icy. Looking down it might have been a long way to the bottom or no deeper than a bath – what was I, a scientist? A little anxious now, I started kicking at the water with my foot.

"Mum, Dad?"

No matter how hard I kicked, the water seemed to be rising higher. Was I sinking or was it coming up to get me? Black liquid spilled inside my shoes. The boat tipped to one side and the waves seemed awful close. For the first time I felt something akin to real fear. Where was the right way out? The other side was still a long way away. The cotton wool wouldn't take my weight. The stars were too far away.

"Daddy," I sobbed, crying out into the darkness. "Mummy, Daddy, where are you?"

It was just like that time on the ice, or the time on the wall – the fog, the darkness, the night. But where was my daddy now?

Suddenly there was an enormous ripping sound and the whole boat (boat?) keeled over to one side. When I looked up, I couldn't see stars, just this enormous black wave, towering above me. The wave reared up, the waters rose, and the whole picture was filled with sea. This sea, I thought, this channel!

After that I didn't see anything ever again.

The Sea of Tranquillity

1

The cemetery was much larger than you'd expect for a town this size. It sprawled across an area the size of two huge playing fields, all the way from the old graveyard almost to the foot of Knob Rock. The oldest bit, running along the side of the now boarded up chapel, was a thick tangle of weeds, ivy and tumbledown headstones, the walkways overgrown and the grass allowed to run riot. But as soon as you passed through the new gates everything changed: the rows of tiny markers ran in straight lines from east to west, the walkways were neat and well trimmed, and the gravel carefully tended. There were no trees, no benches. Each headstone was exactly the same size, all made from precisely the same stone as its neighbours. Even the inscriptions seemed identical. Because each marker was so small, only the names and dates had been included, all engraved in the same angular, uniform script. Some had bundles of fresh flowers lying by them, others had potted plants, still others nothing at all. A sign read 'Garden of Remembrance: No Dogs,

No Running, No Ball Games', but there weren't any dogs or little kids anyway.

It took me quite some time to find Mum and Dad's grave. I wandered up and down the regimented lines, trying to remember the number of rows down from the gates, the direction from the water-pump, the exact distance from the brow of the hill. Once in a while I came across a name I thought I recognised – Emil and Enid Mirozek, Bethan Lewis, Ewan Morgan – and when I spotted them I knew I was (more or less) on the right track. Still, for all that it was a good half hour before I finally found them. Their stone was, of course, just the same as all the others: the barest of inscriptions, their names, the date. There weren't any flowers in the holder and I'd forgotten to bring any with me. O Mum and Dad! It's true what Granny Dwyn used to say – a child like me was no treasure. The marker was even tinier than I remembered it, the dates a mere six days apart. I tried to picture the last time I'd seen them – Dad on the bus, Mum in the hospital – but it was all mixed up in my head. I could see the sets – our boat, the hotel (hotel?), the school – but there was nothing I could do about any of it. Mum and Dad's stone was very smooth and very cold; when I touched it, it was like touching time itself. Then my stomach gave a high-pitched whine and I thought, 'Yes, before dinner I should go and see Aunt Bea and Uncle Glyn too…' Aside from a little group of figures over by the far gate, the entire place seemed deserted. It was fairly dark by now and the cemetery was full of shapes, blobs, dribbles. A cold wind blew in from the bay. Gulls reeled and squawked. I zipped up my yellow puffer and went off to look for my beautiful aunt and my naughty uncle, 'cause the gates were closed at five and, um, who would want to be locked up in a place like this?

Their plot was someplace near a meeting of the paths, pretty close to the shed where the groundskeeper kept his tools, but try as I might I could not find it. Confused, I wandered up and down the rows, not realising that all the time I was drifting closer and closer to the little group of mourners, practically falling over them at the end – some old gal in a headscarf, and a younger man and a woman, the guy as round as a bucket, the girl "pale as a virgin's bum" (Uncle Glyn). As they moved to let me past, I noticed the young guy staring at me kind-of strangely; he was about my age, dressed in a kind of sports-top and jacket, with a greasy goatee-beard and a pair of fantastically wide jeans. But why was he gazing at me so intensely? Had we seen each other somewhere before? Ah, how strange it was! Like looking in a mirror at the wrong reflection. In the end the old woman – his mum? – picked up her shopping bag and hobbled back toward the path, leaving Mr All-Sports and his pale girlfriend (girlfriend?) following on behind. But such a stare! Such a gaze! Who could it have been – Wade, Josh, Kieran and his trousers? Whoever it was he was almost at the gates now, and it was too late to call out. What was the point anyway? I mean, what were these figures to me? Blobs, spots, tiny little daubs in the murk…

Yes, black marks, pale lines, strange angular shapes – mm, the chances of finding Aunt Bea and Uncle Glyn seemed pretty slim by now. In the half-light the cemetery looked even more gloomy and oppressive: the monotonous lines, the faceless blocks, the unrelieved regularity of it all… As Dad used to say, "How did it come to this?" Feeling a little lost, I made my way back out to the perimeter wall and tried following it for a while, the wall strangely smooth and featureless – no graffiti, no stains, no nothing. It was very tall and very pale. Only when you touched the plaster did you notice that it seemed to curve slightly, almost as if it were struggling to form some kind of arc or bend. I tried walking with one hand trailing along it – the wall really was remarkably smooth – but if anything it seemed to take me further and further away from the main part of the cemetery, and so, after a while, I started to head back. What else could I do? It was almost five and the fella on the gate would already be standing by the exit, looking at his watch and cursing me under his breath. Why hadn't I managed to get myself here earlier? Why was I always the one left behind? Sweet Aunt Bea/Dear Uncle Glyn/Open your grave/And let me in... With a heavy heart I turned around and started to pick my way back through the gloom, the sound of my footsteps eerily magnified in the dark: one step, two step, half step, stop. It was so dark now I could barely make out the lines.

As I thought, the caretaker and his 'tache were waiting for me by the main gates, stuck there like they'd been glued to their post. The fella gave a gruff, bad-tempered cough, and took out his enormous ring of keys, picking out the fattest, biggest one of all. Evil little troll – what wouldn't I give to pluck his lip? But then, as I watched the squat, fat fella struggle with the lock, I felt a strange, almost unbearable wave of sadness sweep over me. O Mum and Dad! O Bethan, O Grandy, O me! Not only my aunt and uncle, but the whole world of my childhood was locked inside: the games, the fancies, the voices...

For a moment I considered pushing past him and racing back in, but it was all too late: the gates were locked, the key replaced, the troll retired. No, there was no going back now. When I looked back from across the road, the chain was tied, the gates closed as if forever.

2

Only when I started writing my history of the sickness did I realise just how much was missing, how much had fallen in to the void. I mean, I could remember the boat in quite amazing detail – the funnels, the decks, the cramped little cabins – but for the life of me I couldn't recall how we'd got there, the day we set sail, even the actual moment of landing. The hotel we stayed in had mysteriously turned into the hospital I wound up in after I got ill. The two schools seemed mixed up with some kind of deportation centre. Even my sick bed kept moving – from home to the boat to school – just as the snow somehow turned into paint, a kind of paint "blue as a loved one's eyes" (Uncle Glyn).

Yet what should I do? For as Marco Polo said, "I will record my travels as accurately as possible, allowing for neither exaggeration nor fancy nor distortion…" So there was nothing else to do but take up my pen and write, write about Bethan and Dr Kutchner and Able Seaman Able (the one with the horrible hands), and about Dr Beedie and Mr Carver and Miss Bedford – the only one of my teachers who ever showed me any tenderness – and Hwyl and the wolves and Grandpa's house and everything – and then place it in an envelope, like placing a man in the ground, and post it to Michael, sensible Michael, my brother the scientist… for who would understand my history if not him?

Yes I wrote and wrote and after a while I was there again: back amongst the craters, the lakes, those endless nights, and that strange white hotel in the strange blue snow. And when I'd pieced together all those pictures in the fog, folded back the edges and stuck them roughly in my pad, I pressed the pages down, scrunched the sheets together and sent them off to Michael, my brother Michael, the smartest brother who ever lived…

Before setting off I gave my brother a call from the public phone box in the lobby. The connection was pretty bad but Michael's voice was just the same as always.

"Michael? Is that you?"

"On my phone – who else? Where are you? Are you okay?"

"Sure, sure. Um, I'll come over and see you – I don't know, six-ish, if that's okay? I might stop and try and see Mum and Dad first…"

"Mum and Dad?" There was a pause. "Right."

"Mikey? Is that okay?"

"No, no, that's fine. You haven't forgotten how to find me have you?"

"No, s'okay."

"You won't get lost…"

"No, no…"

"Good."

There was a long gap and I didn't know whether to say anything; still, I couldn't help but ask.

"Michael, did you get it? My manuscript, I mean."

"Manuscript?"

"The envelope…"

There was an even longer pause.

"Michael? Michael, are you there?"

"I'm here Alex."

"Did you get it? The thing I posted to you…"

Another pause.

"Yes Alex, I got it."

"Really? You got it okay? Have you read it? I mean I know it was pretty long and you didn't have much time…"

"No, I've read it Alex."

"Right."

Somebody shuffled right past the phone and I cradled the receiver in my elbow.

"And?"

"And what?"

"What do you think?"

"What do I think?"

I could hear Michael breathing, could almost see his face. But what kind of face was it?

He sighed. "To be honest Alex, I think it's the stupidest thing I've ever read in my life."

All of a sudden the crackling on the line became very bad – like millions of ball bearings hitting a wall. I held the ear piece away from me for a second and then slowly put it back.

"Right."

There was another awkward gap – "Why the long paws?" as Uncle Glyn would say.

"Alex? Alex are you still there?"

"Mm."

"You okay?"

"Mm."

"Well – I'll see you tomorrow then."

"O-okay."

"Till tomorrow…"

"Sure. Good night Michael."

"G'night Alex."

And with that he hung up. My brother, the critic! I listened to the dialling tone for a while and then went to pack my bags: just two pieces per person…

3

Ho, what can I say? Our town seemed as grey and deserted as the moon. The usual discount stores, charity shops, cut-price retail dumps – ah, how boring they looked, how ugly! Drab signs, dull pedestrianised zones, vast swathes of empty office space – like the setting of a play no one would ever put on. *Ych a fi!* As Grandy would have said, "Have you died or were you always that colour?" The bus took the high road past my school then turned left at the roundabout, following the road that ran alongside the playing fields and the dump. It was like the whole thing had been cobbled together from kit-form: stuff unglued, bits missing, the instructions either torn-up or gone. "Who built this anyway – the firm of Bugger and Bodge?" (Dad). One push and the whole lot would fall down: the traffic lights, the betting shops, the nail-bar...

A few lost souls drifted about from shop to shop, but even for a damp, miserable afternoon, the place was pretty quiet. A little light traffic, the occasional taxi, a slow lumbering school bus: even the streets seemed oddly subdued, shuttered windows drooping closed. I was glad when I finally looped my way down to the front, catching sight of its gloomy shelters, run-down arcades, its long line of chip-shops; but even this familiar view was marred by the sight of bland apartment-blocks, anonymous flats, the shell of a hotel complex. "Empty as a policeman's hat" (Uncle Glyn). Only the sea-wall stayed the same: high, black, slippery. And beyond? Why, the heavy, muddied beach, shingles, quicksand, a dirty bathtub of water… 'Yes,' I thought, 'this is it, the murk, the fog, the grey…' No point putting ten pence in the telescope here! On one side the dull puddle of the bay, on the other the rude shadow of Knob Rock, even that surrounded by a circle of thick metal mesh. I know, I know: barriers, barricades, enclosures… The mist (grey, not blue) formed a second wall beyond the sea-defences, a cordon one could never climb over or tunnel under or even chip away at. And worse still it stretched over the sky too, like being inside a great grey sack or a huge pipe, a telescope turned to a vast blind eye…

Before going on to the cemetery I loitered up by the hill for a bit, gazing out over the town, and the sea. There wasn't much to see though: grey banks of cloud moved in restlessly from the bay, great wetting swirls of drizzle and fret, turning everything damp and indefinable. Such gloom! Such fog! Even inland, a drab, heavy wash obscured the gorse-topped hills, the wind-farms and the pylons… Were there really roads leading out, carriageways, railway lines, even a motorway some miles to the east? From where I was sitting, it seemed impossible to imagine anything besides this: the fog, the wall, our tiny circle of familiar ground. Everything else seemed obliterated by the fog, rubbed out as if it had never existed. Ah me! Maybe Michael had been right: "the farthest you can travel is right around the clock…"

Anyway it was pretty late by now and I had to go: the cemetery closed at five and I promised Michael I'd be there by six. It wasn't long before I spotted the way to the graveyard; the wall was very pale and very smooth. I followed it for a while, thinking (if I'm being honest) more about Mikey than those ensconced within. Why had he been so weird on the phone? Why had he said those things? True, we'd never really spoken about what had happened – the sickness, the epidemic, Mum and Dad – but I'd always assumed that he'd come through it all unscathed: no symptoms, no blemishes, no nothing. I know, I know… my brother the enigma! But apart from those "planted in the cabbage-patch" (Grandy) he was the only family I had left. And what could one do without family? "You can't fill a house with only one chair" (Granny Mair).

The first thing I saw when he opened the door was his beard – not a pale, wispy thing, but a great shaggy coat, hanging all the way down from his chin.

"Mikey?"

"Alex?"

We stared at each other like at least one of us was in the wrong place.

"Michael, I…"

"Come in, come in…"

Aside from the hair growth, little else had changed. The carpet, the wallpaper, the hall – everything was just about the same, as if it'd been put together by decorators who'd heard of our place but never actually seen it.

"Those your bags?"

"Um, yeah. I'm travelling light…"

"So I see. What's in that one, a pair of pants and a toothbrush?"

"Toothbrush?"

"Never mind. Here, I'll take it up to your room…"

"Thanks, thanks…"

As I followed him up the stairs I couldn't stop myself from staring at that beard: so long, so bristly, so hirsute! But where had it come from? For some reason I found my brother's newfound woolliness profoundly disturbing. I mean, why had he done it? What did it mean? From where I was standing it was like a passing child had stuck it on for a joke.

My room was just the same as always – beige walls, green blankets, minutely detailed paintings of steam trains and ocean liners on the walls.

"Thanks."

"It's alright. You wash your hands and I'll finish getting dinner ready…"

"Okay…"

"But give them a proper scrub, you hear?"

"Yeah."

"I mean with soap."

"Okay."

As soon as he'd gone I lay down on my bed and stared up at the ceiling. A long straggly cobweb stretched from the light-shade to the window, its strands shaggy with dust. The pictures alongside it were both kind-of faded. In one, a huge black engine emerged angrily from a pitch-black tunnel, wreathed in steam and fog; next to it a giant boat (ship!) could be seen crossing a dark and endless sea, waves crashing and prow rising, its funnels and decks lit by an eerie grapefruit moon. What a vision! What a sight! And all the time I could sense the strong smell of mince creeping up those stairs…

"Are you washing those hands?"

"Um, yeah, sure."

My brother, the yeti!

Michael was surprisingly animated during dinner, talking about school inspections, promotion possibilities, exam grades. I found a long brown hair in my mince but I didn't say anything.

"More gravy?"

"M'okay."

I kept expecting Mikey to ask me about where I'd been and what it was like there but instead he kept going on about the paperwork he had to do, the forms to be filled, the marking.

"Mikey?" I said, skewering a big piece of potato. "Do you ever go out to the cemetery?"

"Sure," he said evenly. "Of course I do."

He paused.

"Did *you* go there?"

"Yeah, well, just for a bit…"

"And?"

"I tried looking for Aunt Bea and Uncle Glyn but it was kind-of dark. In the cemetery, I mean."

"Right…"

"I bumped into this guy there and he gave me the strangest look…"

"Mm," Mikey nodded and pointed at my plate with his fork. He had an enormous chunk of mince caught in his fuzz. "Well…"

"But this guy…"

"Shh…"

How like Dad Michael had become! Sad eyes, furrowed brows, hairy hands. Whilst somehow I had become Mum: abstracted, absent, lost in the snows of Russia…

"Is it funny living here again Mikey? I mean, being back in this place, in this town."

"Funny? Funny how?"

"I mean… living near the sea, being so close to the bay. Have you been down there Mikey, down to the sea-wall?"

"Sure, Alex, I…"

"Just sit on the wall, stare out at the bay, the fog?"

"Well, I suppose…"

"But do you ever see anything Mikey? I mean, if you really stare, stare as hard as you possibly can…"

Mikey was looking at me intently now, his tired eyes smouldering.

"See? See what?"

"See… I don't know. A ship, a boat, maybe? A glimpse of the other side…"

"What do you mean Alex?"

"I don't know… just staring out to sea, waiting for a boat, a ship… something to take you across the bay, across the water…"

I felt my voice starting to break.

"You know, back, back to…"

"Oh Alex," Mikey said softly. We both looked down at my empty plate. The gravy had left a funny looking stain.

"Are you finished? Do you want any dessert?"

"Um, sure, thanks…"

"If you can manage it…"

I tried smiling, "Hey, you know me – I can always make room for the mayor!"

"*That* I can believe…"

Pudding was some kind of trifle, plopped out from a plastic pot. It was a little grey, but otherwise okay. I'd stopped off at a Spar on the way here and bought a bottle and some After Eights, so we had those to finish.

"Just take one, Alex."

"What? Oh, right, sure…"

By this stage we'd moved from the kitchen to the living room, Michael shepherding me to my seat like a sheepdog. The lounge was stuck in the same time warp as the rest of the house: dated decorations, outmoded ornaments, odd bits of furniture. The taped-up timetables and piles of text-books seemed the only original additions.

"I've just got some marking to do. D'you want to see if there's anything on TV while I finish?"

"Um, sure, if you like…"

When I reached for the remote I saw that it was sitting on a big brown envelope, carefully slit open at one end. I looked at Michael and Michael looked at me.

"It's okay, it won't distract me…"

"No, right…"

"You can watch anything you like…"

"Okay, thanks."

I couldn't make out much of what was happening on the TV – something about a vet, I think. Instead I kept glancing at my manuscript. I wasn't sure but it looked like there was a big coffee ring and some working out scribbled on the top.

"You okay Alex?"

"Fine."

"I won't be long."

"S'okay."

Michael stared knowingly into each exercise book as if gazing into his students' very souls. He still had bits of dinner in his chops though.

"Mikey, that mince – was it beef? I mean, it…"

"Alex? Alex, I'm trying to finish this."

"Right, sorry. I'll be quiet."

Somebody seemed to have her arm inside a cow on TV but the sound was very low. The envelope containing my manuscript lay between us, lying on top of a copy of *Continental Modeller* in the magazine-rack.

"If you want to change channels then go ahead…"

"It's alright."

"I won't be long."

"S'okay."

As he marked a long pink tongue came out from between his beard to lick the top of his pen. Embarrassed, I looked away and gazed at the various ceramic birds, train plates and horse brasses hung around the place. How strange it all was: home and yet not home, all at the same time. Had Michael bought up our original furniture or sought out their mates? I wanted to ask but didn't dare disturb him. It was pretty stuffy in there and the minutes stuck together like glue. How long would he be? His red pen scratched away at page after page, occasionally flying back up to his mouth, and those sore, chapped lips. My brother the scholar! Then, just as the vet programme finished, Mikey gathered together his papers, piled the exercise books in one neat tower, and popped the top back on his pen.

"Shall we do the washing-up?"

"Okay."

"You feel well enough?"

"Sure – why wouldn't I?"

"C'mon then."

When we walked through to the kitchen, he seemed uncharacteristically distant, absent almost, away "gathering wool from the clouds" (Mum). His eyes looked sore and his lips awfully blistered. I watched him carefully wipe out the inside of a glass, seemingly lost in thought, and thought, 'Oh my brother – you too?'

"Alex?"

"Mm."

"You know in your story? Why did you write it so we left on a boat?"

"Story?"

"You know, your story, your book…" (An image of me plucking the beard from his chin suddenly popped into my head.) "Why did you have us leaving on a boat?"

"A boat? Well, that's what happened, that's why."

For a second his eyes seemed extraordinarily melancholy – the very same eyes as Dad's.

"Mm," he said. "I see."

"And what does that mean?"

"Mean?"

"C'mon Michael, what are you trying to say?"

Silence.

"You must remember it: the boat, the crossing, the dances in the ballroom…"

Michael looked across at me, his expression almost angry. "A boat, Alex? How's a boat supposed to dock in our little town? Have you

206

been down to the beach recently? There's six feet of mud and two feet of water. How do you think a boat is supposed to moor in that?"

I scrunched up my tea towel and looked down at the sink.

"Well, okay, maybe we caught it further along the coast or something, but I definitely remember a boat…"

"There was no boat Alex…"

"How can you say that? Of course there was a boat – what else?"

Again: those sad eyes (and that meaty-beard!)

"When they first quarantined the town, they took us to the centre on coaches – buses. But of course you were only little so you don't remember…"

"What are you saying? I remember fine. I remember Aunt Bea dancing with Seaman Able, you playing chess with Dr Kutchner, Bethan and I finding Grandy below deck…"

"Alex, Grandy never went with us. We went to visit him in hospital, remember? He was already pretty sick by then…"

"Yeah, I know…" I muttered.

"It's funny though, I'd forgotten all about Dr Kutchner – I used to play chess with him in the recovery ward. Of all the people in the hospital, I wonder why you happened to remember him."

"It was on the boat…"

Mikey shook his head slowly.

"No Alex, you've got it all wrong. I didn't meet Dr Kutchner until we got to the san…"

"Mikey, you weren't even with me when I found Grandy – it was Bethan and I who found him in the hold…"

"Bethan?"

"The girl on the boat!"

"Alex, there was no boat."

"The boat where you met Mabel…"

"Oh yeah, the girl with the pig-tails." Michael grinned. "I mean, it was nice of you to give me a girlfriend and all Alex, but this stuff

– you know that it's just in your head…"

For a full thirty seconds I didn't know what to say. Why was Mikey saying such things? What was he trying to say?

"The girl who was always mooning after you, the girl you ended up with in Big School…"

"Alex, there was no Mabel. There was no boat. I don't know about any Bethan, but if you did meet her it must have been at the special school or the sanatorium…"

"And Dr Beedie and the hairy stewards and the captain?"

"You mean the captain with the ship-shaped hat?"

I glanced at his big hairy face and suddenly wanted to slap him.

"Yes, the ship-shaped hat…"

"And that's what ship's captains wear is it?"

All of a sudden I felt like I was just going to cry. "Forget it then Michael. Just forget the whole thing…"

"Come on Alex, don't get upset…"

"No, let's just drop it…"

"Alex…"

"If you're not interested, then…"

"Alex? Hey, Alex, it's okay…"

"I know what I know: if you want to think something else then that's up to you."

"You were only little Alex. That's why everybody told you we were going on a holiday, that we'd won the special tickets…"

Mikey put down his cloth and put one hand on my shoulder. It seemed very large.

"We didn't want to scare you Alex. Everyone was worried about the sickness. I had to promise not to tell…"

"But the boat…"

"Alex, there wasn't a boat. You're getting it all mixed up with later. We went to the sanatorium in buses…"

"Buses?"

"Yeah. And it certainly wasn't snowing – if anything it was kind-of wet…"

I didn't know what to say. My whole body was trembling. Mike's hands were *really* big.

"You've just got the centre and the hospital all mixed up. It's only natural – you were very small and weren't so well yourself…"

"Mm."

"I mean, you get lots of things right: the wards, the garden, the fence…"

How full Mikey's beard was! Like a great privet hedge. I stared into the greasy water in the sink and tried not to cry.

"So how far away was this camp?"

"I don't know… ten miles, maybe? It was pretty rough and ready but all the hospitals were full so they moved us into this, this… I don't know, some kind of centre or compound, an old holiday camp maybe…"

"And that's where Dad got sick?"

"That's where Dad got sick."

"And Mum?"

"Well… let's not talk about Mum right now. C'mon, let's go and sit in the lounge…"

"D'you think Mum ever found him? I mean, when she went off into the snow…"

"Alex, Mum wasn't very well…"

"No, but…"

"When Dad collapsed, she… she didn't take it so well, Alex. I mean, she knew she had the sickness too…"

"But…"

"Let's not talk about Mum. Come on Alex, come and sit down…"

"Sit?"

"Sit."

The next thing I knew I was back on my chair. It was as if a pair of enormous hands had picked me up and carried me to the lounge. The music on the TV was very pretty but awfully far away. Michael's eyes seemed ringed by a red felt-tip.

"Mikey? Did Dad get sick after falling in at the lake?"

"No, no, the lake thing was ages before... the previous Christmas, maybe. I'm amazed you can even remember it. But it was by no means as dramatic as you made out. I mean, your foot went in and then Dad pulled you out: that's it."

I narrowed my eyes and stared at his chops: could any of this stuff be true?

"And the sea-wall?"

"I don't remember but, um, I wouldn't be surprised: I mean, you were a pretty weird kid..."

"Mm."

I fell silent. My manuscript was still there, big round coffee-stains on it like craters on the moon. Mike's eyes we're just like Dad's: sober, concerned, weary.

"Alex? Alex, I know that it's hard talking about this stuff. The things that happened, the sickness..."

I looked down at my trainers but didn't say anything.

"But this stuff you've written... they're just children's stories Alex, just nonsense..."

"Mikey..."

"Wolves, monsters, trees with fingers instead of branches – they're picture-books, Alex, a kind of fever..."

"Mm..."

My trainers seemed to have trailed some kind of muck all over Mikey's carpet but neither of us mentioned it. Mikey's face seemed very near now. I could see his tongue going in and out, constantly darting out to lick his sore lips.

"I guess..."

"You've got it all mixed up with those books you always had your nose in. You know, you're just like Mum, two peas in a pod…"

When I looked closer at the stains they looked like big blue footprints but I didn't say anything. Someplace bells rang and engines hummed.

"There's a good lad. There's a clever boy…" Mikey whispered.

I nodded absent-mindedly and stared down at the blue.

"A handsome lad, eh? Plenty of miles in you yet…"

Mikey smiled and licked his lips.

"Sir?"

"And a strong boy to boot…"

I nodded and rubbed my palms on the green, scratchy fabric. My nose was running and my neck felt kind of sweaty.

"There's just one thing, my lad. One little thing I've often wondered about. A smart boy like you should be able to tell me, eh? A clever boy with his legs flush to the ground…"

The fabric prickled and rubbed.

"Just one tiny thing. Nothing a lad like you couldn't tell me…"

"Sir?"

Michael squeezed the end of his fleece into a point and for a second I thought it was going to come off.

"What really happened with you and that boy?"

"Boy?"

Mikey (Mikey?) stared at me intently but I couldn't think what he meant.

"Mm, the boy you ran away with. Hwyl, was it? A little scrap of a boy…"

"Hwyl?"

Mikey stared at me hungrily, his red eyes burning. Behind his chair a big pile of boxes were arranged to make some kind of make-shift bed.

"Yes, my lad, Hwyl. Tell me now: how did you and your little friend sneak out? It's all right, you can tell me. A lot of water has flowed under the bridge since then, eh? Don't worry, lad, you can't get into trouble now."

My mouth opened and closed like a fish. His face seemed very close and very big.

"That night you ran away, d'you remember? What did you do at the big fence, my boy? How did you get over?"

I wanted to say something but for some reason nothing seemed to come out.

"Eh, my lad? How did you manage to climb out? Was there somebody helping you?"

Silence.

"What happened to your little friend?"

"He... went back," I said. "After he fell down the crater he wouldn't play with me anymore, so he said he was going back..."

And for a second I could even see him: his funny, scrawny body, bandy little legs, strange egg-shaped head...

"And did you really walk all the way home on your own? All the way to town?"

"I don't know... I mean, I remember a building site, a half-built house, reaching some huge wall..."

"A wall?"

The doctor patted his beard like a dog. Behind him, in the walls, something hummed and swayed.

"Mm, some kind of wall or enclosure, something cutting me off from the other side..."

"Ah..."

"And this wall, this barrier, it went on and on, without mark or stain or sign of any kind..."

"And yet you got through?"

I stared hard at the big blue marks. "I don't know how to explain it. It wasn't so much I got through – more I found myself looking at it from the opposite side..."

"And then you were back in our town?"

"Mm…"

"You'd walked all the way back home…"

"Yeah – well, I don't know. Everything seemed so flimsy and dilapidated. It was both our town and not our town – d'you understand? Even though I'd managed to get through, nothing was the same, nothing was right… and then after I'd gone through, after passing that wall… well, suddenly there was no way back…"

The fella's great mouth opened and for a second I was worried he might eat me.

"Back?"

"You know? From the other side…"

I closed my eyes and felt his beard tickle my cheek.

"Oh Alex," said a voice – Dr Beedie? Mikey? Dad? "Oh Alex, why do you say these things? You know as well as I do – there is no other side."

4

When I opened my eyes again Michael was gone – and with him the smell of mince. My head throbbing I made my way over to the window and watched the fog blotting out the houses one by one. The mist lapped at the parked cars, the quiet road, the long black fingers of the tree. 'Fog, fog, fog,' I thought. How mysterious it was, how unknowable! Like the sickness, the bay, the past…

Behind me I could hear something footering about, but I stayed where I was, my eyes fixed on that long, grey curtain of mist. How deep it was, how impenetrable! The mist rubbed away at the shapes and colours till there was nothing left, the merest trace of an unremembered night…

The fog was really very close now. The street, the wall, the tree – all gone, replaced by a kind of wash or stain, some kind of great grey sea. When I stared through the window I could almost make out my own features – an eye, half a mouth, a little red ear floating in space. Then these too started to fade and all I could see was mistiness, "half a spoon of nothing…"

Though I didn't want to go to bed, I did feel pretty tired. I reached round and dragged Mikey's chair over to the window, knocking over his carefully arranged marking in the process. The chair was very saggy and very big and as I relaxed into the cushion, an enormous feeling of well-being – of tranquillity, even – started to come over me. My limbs relaxed and my head start to loll. At last, I thought – the softest straw in the stall! But then, just as my eyelids started to flicker and my breathing began to slow, I heard it: a long protracted lowing, the

long, slow, drawn-out call of a horn, a sound from the beginning of
time itself. What a sound, what a wail! I imagined some prehistoric
creature raising its head cautiously out of the fog, its yellow eyes all
doleful and sad. But there again, maybe it was nothing of the sort –
maybe it was just the lonely, mournful siren of a ship, some vast, rusty,
cockle-encrusted ferry, carrying its passengers who knew where…

Then all of a sudden I could actually see it: the boat's long, andeluvian
flank, its three tall chimneys, the lighting and the lifeboats….

No, not a dinosaur but a vast black ship, tall as a mountain, long
as a clock tower turned on its side. Ah, what a mighty vessel! Such a
thing! Its keel was as wide as the car park by our school, the hull as
long as the sea-wall at the front, its decks as high as the transmitter
on Knob Rock…

Above it, coal-black soot from the chimneys mixed with the soft grey
nothingness of the fog, creating a kind of scuffed charcoal drawing,
half-there, half-not, its shape blotted against the eternal darkness of
the sea. O my ship! O my ferry! As it cut its way across our garden I
could almost smell it: the fumes, the oil, the salt. Sure it looked a little
rusted – one of the masts starting to lean and a couple of lifeboats
missing from the deck – but still: how could one's heart not beat just
a little faster? Its prow filled up the window, its side bigger than the
house…

Right next to me I could see stick-like figures running to get their
coats, their shapes darting up and down ladders, along observation
points, poking through portholes. Lanterns were lit, whistles were
blown, and the tiny dots started to gather together near the cabins,
metal filings pulled by some kind of irresistible force. Yes, they were
nearly there now – we were *all* nearly there now – landfall, *terra firma*,
our final destination…

And high above the ship, the waves, tch, even above the fog itself,
turned a green and blue globe, beautiful, luminous, an enormous
ball spinning amongst the stars. And that's when I knew how far I'd

come – the feet, the miles, the years…

And after all that to end up here, marooned on this lifeless shore, on this moon, this shell. Ho, how empty it all seemed! Deserted streets, hollow houses, beaches made of dust not sand… Without even knowing it, I'd passed over, scaled that featureless wall, travelled unwittingly from one world to the next. Why hadn't I realised? Why hadn't I known? The true, kind earth floated clear and pure amongst the stars and the sea and I thought, 'Yes, that's right, I've always known it: childhood, beauty, that other shore…' And then the ship's horn blew and I knew that this would be the last time I'd hear it – that call, that echo, that deep booming basso…

Listen: the world turned, the fog roiled, the stars swam. But when I looked back at the room, nothing had changed. The chair, the table, the scattered notebooks on the floor – all were exactly as before. It was pretty dark. Most of the things were kind-of indistinct, but then, amongst the textbooks and pencils, I spotted something I hadn't seen before, something flat and fuzzy, stretched out on a table as if to dry. Cautiously I reached out a hand then withdrew it: jiw jiw, was that Mikey's beard? It lay on a little white saucer, looking strangely thin and limp, the edges curling up a bit where they'd become unglued. What was it? My hand hovered over the fur for a moment but then I sat back down in the chair again. No, I thought, not yet… The whiskers didn't move and I didn't want to touch them. Instead I gazed longingly back at the window, looking for my ship, my globe, my friends the stars…

What's that? What was I waiting for? Tch, who knows the answer to such things? I was waiting for the fog to lift, for the morning to come, for the sickness to pass. All I know is that I stayed in the chair for a very long time.

About the Author

ALAN BILTON was born in York in 1969. In keeping with the two main sources of employment back then, his family either worked on the railways or in chocolate. Unlike his more practical and mechanically-minded brothers, he became neither a surveyor nor a train-spotter. Rather, he received his undergraduate degree in Literature and Film from Stirling University in 1991, and his PhD (for a study of Don DeLillo, an author with whom he has absolutely nothing in common in any way) from Manchester University in 1995. He then taught American Studies at Liverpool Hope University College and Manchester University before moving to take up a post teaching literature and film at Swansea University in 1996. He is married, with one small child and one hairy dog. His first novel, *The Sleepwalkers' Ball*, described by one critic as 'Kafka meets Mary Poppins', was published by Alcemi in 2009. He is also the author of books on silent film comedy, contemporary fiction, and America in the 1920s, alongside short stories, essays and reviews. He teaches Creative Writing, fiction and film at Swansea.

www.AlanBilton.co.uk

Lightning Source UK Ltd.
Milton Keynes UK
UKOW03f0255040314

227471UK00001B/1/P